Bitter Gets Better

BITTER GETS BETTER

DONTE W. FORD

AuthorHouse™
1663 Liberty Drive
Bloomington, IN 47403
www.authorhouse.com
Phone: 1-800-839-8640

© 2012 by Donte W. Ford. All rights reserved.

No part of this book may be reproduced, stored in a retrieval system, or transmitted by any means without the written permission of the author.

Published by AuthorHouse   12/04/2012

ISBN: 978-1-4772-8175-8 (sc)
ISBN: 978-1-4772-8172-7 (hc)
ISBN: 978-1-4772-8174-1 (e)

Library of Congress Control Number: 2012919596

Any people depicted in stock imagery provided by Thinkstock are models, and such images are being used for illustrative purposes only.
Certain stock imagery © Thinkstock.

This book is printed on acid-free paper.

Because of the dynamic nature of the Internet, any web addresses or links contained in this book may have changed since publication and may no longer be valid. The views expressed in this work are solely those of the author and do not necessarily reflect the views of the publisher, and the publisher hereby disclaims any responsibility for them.

Dedication

As a little boy, I can remember my mother "Shirley E. Ford" embracing, enduring, accepting and facing many struggles in life. I never knew what any of those words meant, but today as a man I appreciate and love my mother dearly for singly raising myself and four other siblings. Mother, you are the best mom in the world, and this book is dedicated to you. I love you!

About the Author

As featured in the 2012 Fourth Edition of Who's Who in Black Charlotte, Author-Donte W. Ford is an assistant manager of the historic Excelsior Club. The nation's oldest running African-American social institution. Mr. Ford is the founder and chief executive officer of Concerned Father's Unlimited, an organization that coaches single fathers into strong, responsible fatherhood. Donte volunteer's his time through various community groups and organizations throughout Mecklenburg County and surrounding areas.

Donte is an award-winning mixed martial artist, and mentor. As one way to relieve stress, he instructs a Free Urban Beginner's Ballroom

Dance once a week. One of his honor's and achievements is having a small cameo in the 1986 movie "Colors" starring Sean Penn and directed by the late Dennis Hopper.

Donte was acknowledged by the United Way of Boston for carrying the Olympic Torch in the 1996 Olympic Games in Atlanta, Ga.

In 1997, he received the "Black Rose Award" for Outstanding Commitment to the Positive Advancement of African-American people by the Kappa Nu chapter of Sigma Gamma Rho Sorority, Inc. In 2007, he was acknowledged by Coca-Cola for Teacher Assistant of the month at Metro School. He is also an active life-time member of Iota Phi Theta Fraternity, Inc.

A native of Los Angeles now living in Charlotte, NC by way of Boston, Donte W. Ford was educated at Burdett Business School and Boston College. He is a single active dad of Noah and Alyssa Ford, who are the center of his life. Donte is very excited as a new author! He has a lot to share, so he request for you to follow his new passion and to come build with him at Donte's Place (website). Donte appreciates and is thankful for any support you provide.

P.S. In Donte's words, "Always follow your desires and dreams and let know body put out your flame or steal your joy. Keep smiling knowing you own and control your destiny. I'm with you so let's get it done. Let's go!"

Acknowledgments

First and foremost, I thank my heavenly Father and his son, Jesus Christ. Without God, none of my achievements would be possible.

I thank my beautiful and hardworking mother, Shirley E. Ford, for grooming me into the man I am today. Mother, you deserve so much more, and on behalf of my siblings and me, we love you dearly.

I thank my sister Teresa and my brother Larry for always encouraging me to reach for the stars. I thank my sister Nichie, my brother Richard and younger brother William DeBruce for supporting me and keeping me strong. I love you all.

I thank my beautiful daughter, Alyssa, and my handsome son, little Donte (Noah), for giving me a new direction in life. It's hard, children, but Daddy is not giving up. Daddy wants you guys to find it within your hearts to provide and be strong for your families and give back to society.

I thank Dennis Adams of Omega Psi Phi Fraternity, Inc. and Kalonji Bartee of Iota Phi Theta Fraternity, Inc. for investing and believing in me. Thank you, brothers.

I thank Dr. Dorothy Webb-Moody for all her shared time, wisdom, and support. Thank you, Dr. Dorothy Webb-Moody.

I thank Dr. Sharon Patterson for her support, shared time, and inside guidance. You are a best-selling author, and I respect you greatly.

I thank Dr. Shalair Armstrong for her time, encouraging words, and support. You have been a true friend since our teenage and college days. I am so proud of you for your achievements.

I thank Allister Charles (AC) for being a true friend and for thinking out of the box. Keep doing what you do and let no one tell you anything different.

I thank Senator Charles Dannelly for his encouragement, wisdom, shared time, support letters, speaking engagements, and kind words. Senator Dannelly, there will never be another senator to come along and replace you. You are the best one to do it.

I thank Walter Brewer for his words of encouragement, believing in me and telling me that I'm great. For telling me to let no man or woman discourage me from doing me. A big thumbs-up, Walter—or should I say Governor?

I thank Stan Frazier, author of the history book *Maroons*, for his direction, shared time, and support. You are a best-selling author as well. I appreciate you and respect you greatly. Stan, thanks for being a big brother and helping to lead me to the fountain. I will continue drinking.

I thank Francetta Farrer, Publisher & Chief Executive Officer *The County News* for her words of wisdom, shared time, support, and community dedication, and for keeping our communities informed about me (smile).

I thank Lorenzo, "Big Ren," for support, shared words, and calling it like it is, which is "keeping in touch with my feminine side." Big Ren, it's okay for masculine men to write as well.

I thank Taj Ferguson for his shared time, community outreach, and fatherhood support with Concerned Fathers Unlimited. I also thank you, Taj, for lending your listening skills.

Again, I thank Mr. Kalonji Bartee for being a true fraternity brother and friend. Frat, I thank you for upholding the true essence of fraternity brotherhood. In your words: "Frat, you know how we do."

I thank the entire staff of Auto Care Center on Freedom Drive in Charlotte for upholding great professionalism in a working environment and for keeping my vehicle serviced and on the road.

Finally, I thank all my supporters, associates, and friends for being true to me as a person. Thank you for helping me make my first novel what it is today.

I love you all, and again, thank you!

Contents

Dedication v

About the Author vii

Acknowledgments ix

Chapter 1: I'm Sheryl. It's All about Me, Myself, and I 1

Chapter 2: Friendship and Truths 15

Chapter 3: Store 24: A Woman's Challenge 26

Chapter 4: Mistaken Identity 54

Chapter 5: The Proposal 129

Chapter 6: The Shopping Spree 155

Chapter 7: The Rehab 185

Chapter 1

I'm Sheryl. It's All about Me, Myself, and I

I'm Sheryl Bates, and this is my story. It takes place in an old city that I have come to know and love. This old city is Boston. I love the diversity and the culture. It's the birthplace of the American Revolution. It's the home of historic institutions for higher learning, such as Harvard, MIT, Wentworth, and Boston College, to name a few.

Although I received and accepted a full academic ride to attend Brown University in Providence, Rhode Island, Boston is now my home.

The day is Saturday and it's a nice spring afternoon. My best friend from college, Angie Coleman, and I are coming back from last-minute shopping for an event this evening.

Tonight at the Park Plaza Hotel and Towers in downtown Boston, an organization called Concerned Fathers Unlimited (CFU) will meet. This is a support group and web-based site for single fathers who are active in their children's lives. They are hosting their fifth annual Autism Awareness fund-raiser.

Angie and I have been supporting this event for the past four years, and it seems to get better each year we attend. It's a two-hundred-dollar-per-plate social that donates its profits to various autism schools and agencies throughout the Boston area.

At this fund-raiser two years ago, Angie met her dog of a boyfriend. Roland Diaz is his name.

I can't wait to be seated. I'm excited. I'm just waiting to see who our special guest will be.

Over the years we've been surprised with performers like Bell Biv Devoe, Justin Timberlake, Tony Braxton, and Neo. Talk about a fun time for a great cause . . .

We already have our hair done. I had to get my nails refilled, Angie got her eyebrows arched, and I finally picked up my BCBG black pumps.

I just came back from buying a black, one-shoulder-strap, silk chiffon dress and this soft, cherry-red, Dolce & Gabbana fitted blouse. Next Friday, I'm picking up an ivory Chanel dress I saw at Saks Fifth Avenue.

I love shopping. I'm at the malls every chance I get. When I'm bored, depressed, hungry, or lonely, I find myself shopping. Yes, shopping is a weakness for me and one of my favorite pastimes. You should see my closet. I have shoes and clothes I bought three years ago that still have tags on them.

When traveling, I always have mixed feelings regarding my choice of clothing. I sometimes forget to pack one of my favorite outfits and may have problems putting something together.

This is when I get in my Cadillac SUV and head to my shopping spots. A client turned me on to these shops she called the Ten Best. It's a group of stores ranging from independent boutiques to upscale chains. These are the places I go to relax and have my "me time" while getting through my clothing crisis.

Sheryl's Ten Best:

- *Akris*: This is my business suits and shoes spot.

- *Alan Bilzerian*: This is my European connection. It carries European designers such as Ann Demeulemeester, John Galliano, Raf Simons, and Yohji Yamamoto. They carry a little bit of everything.

- *Betsey Johnson*: Now Betsey Johnson is my funky and happily out-of-the-ordinary spot. This is where I get a lot of my dresses, slacks, and innovative jackets.

- *Chanel*: This is one of my favorites. We all know Chanel; it speaks for itself. Here is where I get most of my accessories, like my handbags, fragrances, hats, jewelry, scarves, and shoes.

- ***Emporio Armani***: I really appreciate this store for its fine fabrics. Here is where I get a lot of my well-cut suits, blazers, sportswear, and khakis.

- ***Ermeneqildo Zegna***: I like this spot for my luggage, button-downs, and some of their sportswear.

- ***Max Mara***: This shop is where I primarily build my outfits. I think they have some of the finest in traditional classics. Their dresses, jackets, scarves, and shoes come in a nice spread of pastels and neutrals, made to fit my wardrobe.

- ***Ricardi Boutique***: This spot is where I shop for my nephews, uncles, and other male family members and friends. They have a good selection of the latest gear: European sportswear, jeans, coats, shoes, and accessories.

- ***The Garment District:*** TGD is my vintage and contemporary clothing spot. It's my "alternative department store," selling vintage clothing for a dollar a pound, along with music, party, and pop culture accessories.

- ***Thomas Pink:*** Thomas Pink is the spot for high-quality fabrics and design. They carry bold-colored clothing and well-made, custom-tailored shirts. Thomas Pink is my nightlife and club scene gear.

As you can see, I love shopping. I have a taste of the world right here in Boston. I'm actually adding more space to my closet as we speak. I have clothes and shoes all over my condo. My condo looks like one big closet.

It's about that time to call Goodwill for a pickup. This is a mess. I spoil myself. I try giving Angie brand-new clothes and she will not take them. My girl Angie could not care less about how she dresses. She has a man, and an attitude of "who am I trying to impress?" I can't get her to go shopping with me for anything.

I want to give my girl a makeover because nowadays with Angie, what you see is what you get. In her college days, she was the hottest woman on campus next to me. I think she's stuck in the early 90s. She's still wearing some of those same old jeans and shirts.

What's different about Angie today is the fact that she holds down her job as Detective Coleman. She is one of the top detectives in Boston.

I have everything I want except for a man to call my own. I tell you, it's sad when a woman as fine as I am is sometimes lonely and frustrated. I've met and been introduced to all types of men—married men, thugs, players, and hustlers.

Have you ever met a man who still lives at home with his parents, but claims he wants to buy you the world? He wants to do this and do that, but won't get his own place for some odd reason. What about the boy who is young enough to be your child but still tries to date you? It's just hard to find a good man.

I can't find a man worth investing my time in. I sometimes wonder how Angie got her man. All she does is work, work out, and work. Roland has to be using her for her money. She's not into any fashions; she's a plain Jane. She doesn't drink or smoke, and she hates going out on the town. She's boring. She puts me in mind of Oprah in her movie *The Color Purple*. We're night and day, but that's my girl.

I'm the truth, like a Venus Williams tennis outfit and serve. My measurements are 34C, twenty-nine inches in the waist, and thirty-eight inches in the hips. I have mouthwatering curves in all the right places, and I love to dress in the hottest fashions.

I'm five feet eight inches tall and weigh a toned one hundred and sixty pounds. I have a smooth, rich, chocolate complexion. Look in any dictionary and you'll see a picture of me as the definition of a beautiful black woman.

As I drive my black 2008 Cadillac Escalade, sitting on black twenty-four-inch rims with the Nitto Invo tires, or as I look out of my four-bedroom condo that overlooks the Charles River, I remember when I lived with my mom, two brothers, and two sisters in a small, two-bedroom apartment.

My brothers, sisters, and I had to share the same clothes, shoes, and school supplies for many years. Back then, I thought this day of my independence would never come.

Now I work full time as a certified public accountant for Noah Investments and part time as a fitness instructor for Bodies by Alyssa.

I became the happiest woman in the world when I finally earned my master's in business administration from Brown University in 1996.

If you can imagine, I feel like Whitney Houston in her movie *Waiting to Exhale*—only I needed to exhale yesterday.

The fact remains that I'm still single, and being single at times has its disadvantages. I do maintain. I can always count on a fresh pack of AA Duracell batteries for my toys. However, nothing can replace the warm and safe feeling of being caressed in a spoon position by a strong and sexy man. It's like an infant's need for a security blanket.

Roland brings Angie that kind of completeness, but I'm sure Roland will mess that up. He's a dog like most men, and time will soon catch up with his pretty-boy looks.

Men tell you what you want to hear in the beginning. Then, after they get your sweet kisses and womanhood, the wanting and lusting stops. I'm speaking for all women on this one, because we all have experienced this before.

I'm going to expose that side of Roland before Angie gets lost in his lies. For now, here's more about me and my girl Angie.

We met at track and field practice our sophomore year at Brown University. Angie held the 100—and 200-yard state records. I ran on the relay team with Angie and two other girls, Keisha Gorman and Linda Stalks.

Bitter Gets Better

Back then, we were in the newspaper every week. Angie also held the state indoor fifty-five-yard dash record up until 1993. The record was broken by one of our own, Keisha Gorman.

Angie had a car, she was a proud woman of Sigma Gamma Rho, Sorority, Inc and she won the title of Ms. Community two years in a row from those so-fine brothers of Iota Phi Theta Fraternity, Inc. Ow-Sweet to the men who proudly wear the gilded gold and charcoal brown and are building traditions, not resting upon one!

Angie became popular from track and field, plus she had a body that caused many heads to turn like whoa. She was a criminal justice major, and now she works as a detective for the Boston Police Department. But don't let the popular schoolgirl image of Angie fool you. She also gave the name "Ghetto" a new meaning.

I remember a dorm-room situation one year. She was fighting this guy from the football team named Brian Clark, whom she had a crush on. She was hitting him like Laila Ali in a title fight. Brian had started a rumor about how Angie liked Halls cough drops eaten from her womanhood, and how she liked her hair to be grabbed while in doggy position.

She told me the sex did happen and she actually enjoyed it. The fight was over the fact that Brian was sharing it with the locker room. He was wrong for putting their business out there. I heard people talking about it on a Thursday evening on campus while I was writing an eighty-page history paper in the library.

I can only imagine how Angie felt. We would be around campus or just hanging out in the quad, and dudes would make sexual gestures or come up and say rude things to her. One guy who was about six feet six had the nerve to walk up to her, forcefully grab her ponytail, and say, "Is this how you like it?"

After she punched him in the face and I kicked him in his privates, we reported his actions to campus police. That's also when we went to Brian's dorm room like a gang on a mission and started a fight. There were about eight of us from the track team. We set it off.

I'm glad I was messing around with the quarterback, Michael Bradson, because he made sure other dudes didn't trip. After they heard why Angie was tripping, they understood. Brian and some other football players eventually beat up the guy who grabbed her ponytail.

Angie was upset that whole semester. The mention or sight of Brian made her sick to her stomach.

Dudes need to keep their mouths shut about their personal business. (Some women are guilty of telling their business as well.) Brian, feeling sorry for Angie, started denying that he'd slept with her. From that point on, when he talked about it, he would say that he'd been playing. But by that time the damage was done, and everyone on campus knew about it. Even one of the male math professors gave me some suggestions to share with Angie if she wanted to hear them.

Angie stopped dating for a while. Actually, Roland is the second guy she's dated since then. We have to learn from our mistakes. Some of us get wiser and stronger, and some of us have to learn the hard way. Some men are just not worth the rumors.

Yes, our college days were crazy, and I'm sure you had some wild days as well. Brian is now playing in the NFL. He's been married for three years and has two sons and a daughter.

These days, Angie is five feet seven and weighs about 140 pounds. She's cute, but not as cute as I am. Her measurements are about a 34C, with a thirty-inch waist and I want to say thirty-six in the hips. She reminds me of a taller version of Nia Long, but with longer hair and light-brown eyes.

Now Angie is from Boston, specifically from an inner-city neighborhood called Roxbury in the Grove Hall area. This is the section where Malcolm X lived while he was in Boston, on a street called Warren. It's also where I get my hair done, at a hair salon and barber shop called Reggie's Hair World or "Mattapan's Finest," by a stylist named Nicole.

Angie's the youngest of five and the only girl. She and her oldest brother were the only ones in the family to graduate from a four-year college.

To date, Angie and I are still best friends, but Roland takes up most of her time. I see why they get along so well. Roland is the passive, work all day, "honey I'm home" type. He does hold down a steady job, but Angie could do much better.

Donte W. Ford

She still looks the same from our college days, and now she's even more filled out. I need to get her out of the house and do that makeover, because, as I mentioned, time will soon tell that Roland is a dog.

As for me, I'm a daddy's girl. I'm intelligent, sexy, and fine, but still having difficulties finding a man who is worthy of my time. Men are constantly in and out of my life. I'm tired of hearing the same old excuses and lines . . .

Lines and excuses like, "You're the finest woman I have ever seen." "Excuse me, do you taste as sweet as you look?" "You know what? I lost your number, that's why I haven't called you." And "Don't I know you from somewhere?" Ladies, do we still entertain these lame lines from the cute guys?

The woman that I am gets in the way of my personal life. I know I sound a little vain, somewhat desperate and forward, but I'm just tired of child's play.

I was known by the boys back home as "the stuck-up chick." I never gave guys the time of day; I stayed to myself. I was strictly into school. I knew I wanted to get married and have my own family one day. So I made the choice when I was sixteen not to allow my children to grow up in the same environment that I did.

I remember one early Wednesday morning, going to school, I was at the corner of Firestone and Compton Avenue at the bus stop back home in Los Angeles. I saw three boys get shot up by some gang-bangers in a car.

Bitter Gets Better

Later on the news, I heard that two of the three boys died, and the other one was paralyzed from the waist down. Seeing those boys murdered and injured for life was my green light to get out. I saved my money, got tunnel vision, and moved out of the state. I had to see what life had to offer me outside of Los Angeles. I had to work hard for everything I own. A man can't give me anything unless I want it.

My father made me promise him on my sixteenth birthday to study and handle my business so I could hold my own and do for me. My father told me I should not need a man for anything, other than having a family and maybe networking. My daddy died three days after my sweet-sixteen party from diabetes.

My father is no longer here, but I keep him in my spirit by supporting and volunteering with the American Diabetes Association. I never got the chance to tell my daddy I loved him, but I will always be my daddy's girl. It's about supporting and moving forward—which brings me back to our fund-raiser tonight.

Hundreds of people enjoy going to this fund-raiser every year. It's fun, and I like the networking. Over the years, I've meet all type of professionals: doctors, lawyers, writers, principals, teachers, actors, and singers. This will be my fifth year attending this fund-raiser, and as mentioned, it's held at the Park Plaza Hotel and Towers, which is located in the heart of the historic Back Bay.

This location is one of the area's most recognized landmarks. The Park Plaza Hotel and Towers has fifteen floors. It's a Starwood-managed property and a member of Historic Hotels of America. It opened on

March 10, 1927, as part of the E. M. Statler empire. It is three miles from Logan International Airport and only two hundred yards from the nation's first public parks, Boston Common and the Public Garden. The hotel is easily accessible to shopping—and you know I love to shop.

The hotel is also minutes from Newbury Street, Faneuil Hall Marketplace, and the theater and financial districts. Keep in mind that Newbury Street and Faneuil Hall Marketplace are more great shopping!

Even when there's nothing going on in Boston, tourists come from all parts of the world to stay at the Park Plaza Hotel. Their rooms are a blessed respite from the negative views and sounds of the city.

Every year except for this year, Angie and I have booked the presidential suite. It has its own elevator that stops in the living room. It has three beautiful bedrooms and five bathrooms, a large living room, a private office, and kitchen. There's a sixty-inch flat screen in the living room and a forty-two-inch flat screen in each bedroom. The refrigerator comes stocked with bottled water, assorted juices, sodas, and beer. Plus it has around-the-clock room service.

The bathrooms are marbled, the furniture is leather, and it has a grand piano and a surround-sound stereo system. One day I'll learn how to play the piano, but for now, using it for my sexy and cute pictures works for me.

Even after the fund-raiser is over, I look forward to my one-night stay: going up to my suite, sitting in the hot tub, feeling the jets massage my back and neck, and simply relaxing.

This year Angie and Roland booked our presidential suite. I may or may not stay. I have to see how my night goes with this new guy. Can you believe Roland, Angie's dog of a boyfriend, is trying to hook me up with a friend of his named Earl? Roland is trying to set me up! This should be interesting. I guess he thinks if I get a man, I'll stay out of Angie's ear and their business.

Angie told me Earl is six feet two with dark-brown eyes, and he's built. "Chocolate Thunder with good credit." With a name like Chocolate Thunder, I thought he was a stripper.

I spoke earlier about men being dogs, but I'm due for a fix. Tonight, as long as Earl says the right things to me, my plans are to play it by ear and allow whatever happens to happen. Tonight, I'm feeling free and adventurous!

I don't mean to sound desperate, but there's nothing like long, sweaty, and pounding sex, especially when the last time I had some was approximately eighteen months, three weeks, four days, twenty-six minutes, and five seconds ago! Can you imagine? I will never again deprive myself.

I wonder if Earl is the quiet or shy type. I hope he's not the type of man who's sexy as hell but talks too much. You know the man who has the slamming body and looks good, but talks himself out of the goodies.

Forgive me if I sound aggressive or unladylike, but when 2012 swung around, it was a new year for women, and I'm the new prototype.

Time is near for the fund-raiser and I need to go pick up Angie. Let me call her and tell her I'm on my way.

Chapter 2

Friendship and Truths

As the phone rings at Angie's house, she picks up and says, "Hello?"

Sheryl replies, "Hey girl, what's up? I'm on my way. I'll be there in fifteen minutes. Please be ready."

Angie tells her, "Sheryl, I'm ready now."

Sheryl says, "Okay, I'll be there shortly."

Sheryl arrives at Angie's house. Angie says, "You got here quick."

Sheryl says, "I was already en route when I called you. I'm scared of you, girl—when did you get a breast job?"

Angie replies, "Sheryl, I did not get a breast job. You're silly."

Sheryl tells her, "Your bust has that strapless dress fitting you well, and those black-studded shoes make your calves look like you work out. Turn around, Angie. I'm so proud of you. You look really nice when you decide to dress up."

Angie says, "You know I'm on my Stair Master at least three times a week. I have to look good for my man."

Sheryl asks, "You mean Roland?"

Angie answers, "Whatever, Sheryl. Don't hate. What about you? Can that dress fit you any better? That dress was made for you."

Sheryl asks, "What about these shoes? Should I have worn the black ones instead of these?"

Angie replies, "I like those. They highlight your dress more."

Sheryl says, "We look too good not to be remembered. Is your camera fully charged? Let's do like the kids do and just smile and click."

"You're silly." After taking several pictures, Angie tells Sheryl, "Hold on. I just need to grab my cell, my purse, and the tickets off the coffee table."

Sheryl says, "Make sure you have everything, I would hate to get there and not have the tickets."

Angie says, "Do not start with me."

Sheryl replies, "You remember that Janet Jackson concert we went to when you forgot the tickets? We had to spend another one hundred and fifty dollars each for new tickets."

Angie tells her, "I know, right? That won't happen again. I have the tickets right here."

Sheryl steps outside to get her truck as Angie grabs the tickets and other items. En route to the Plaza, they speak about last year's fund raiser.

Sheryl asks, "Who's the DJ this year?"

Angie replies, "DJ Sweet, the same DJ from last year."

Sheryl says, "She was not good."

Angie says, "Whatever! She was good. Neo just stole the night. Girl, that man Neo can sing."

Sheryl replies, "Neo did do his thing. Is DJ Sweet local?"

Angie says, "I heard she was from New Haven."

Sheryl asks, "Who's from Connecticut?"

Angie replies, "Girl, who knows? But I do hope you and Earl click."

Sheryl says, "I'm sick of these tired men, but as long as there's some shopping and he pampers me. I'll be all right. We'll see if Earl is cool or not. Roland works at AutoZone, right?"

Angie replies, "Here we go. You're in my business."

Sheryl says, "For real, Angie, he does work at AutoZone, right?"

Angie says, "Yes. What's your point?"

Sheryl comments, "You need to leave that man alone. He's broke, and he's not making any real money."

Angie says, "I have a man with a full-time job, and he loves me. Can you say the same?"

Sheryl replies, "He works at AutoZone. Come on, get real. You did not earn your master's degree to end up with a man with just a high school education."

Angie says, "You're right! I received my master's degree for me. Roland is happy at what he does. Like you and I are happy at what we do. That's all that matters. He works and he's committed to me. I like how you continue to preach to me about my man and you have over a dozen toys at home. What's wrong with this picture?"

Sheryl says, "Don't you want a man who can support you?"

Angie replies, "I support myself."

Sheryl asks, "You mean to tell me you don't want a man who can afford to romance you, buy you nice things, and take you on vacations?"

Angie says, "How much money does a man need to hold your hand while walking in the park? Does it really cost a man to open a car door, pull out a chair, or compliment me? I mean, really, how much does romance cost, Sheryl?"

Sheryl replies, "Roland is sprung and weak."

Angie says, "You just don't get it. Do you even know why you're so unhappy?"

Sheryl asserts, "I'm good."

Angie replies, "No, you're not, and you're getting on my damn nerves."

Sheryl says, "Wow! Where did that come from?"

Angie says, "You're always running your mouth. Do you ever listen to yourself? You're selfish. I need to work on you."

Sheryl asks, "Work on me?"

Angie says, "Yes, work on you and your attitude. You're arrogant too. Before you make anyone else happy, you have to be happy with yourself."

Sheryl replies, "I'm happy with me. I don't know what you're talking about."

Angie says, "You are lonely, frustrated, and stubborn. You are mean as well, with a my-way-or-no-way attitude. But I know why you're that way. You need to get you some."

Sheryl repeats, "Get me some?"

Angie answers, "Yes. Get you some real sex and put those toys down for a minute. There's nothing like the real thing. You may think I'm plain Jane, but when I'm heading into work every morning, there's a big Kool-Aid smile across my face."

Sheryl replies, "I can't believe you said that."

Angie says, "Well, it's about time, don't you think?"

Sheryl says, "You're the one who's mean."

Angie replies, "I know you're tired of those cold, hard toys, and of spending your money on those expensive batteries."

Sheryl says, "I'm not messing with you. We were talking about Roland, remember?"

Angie says, "Roland and I are good. It's you with the problem. It's not about Roland being weak or sprung, because he's neither. It's about knowing what I want and need in a man. I prayed for the type of man

I wanted. God sent him, and I will hold on to him. I have a man who appreciates everything he works for, including me. I'd be a fool to give that up for a man who has no substance. We're a team.

"I bet you know nothing about the word team, do you? Don't suck your teeth; it's the truth. Roland is sweet, sincere, and thoughtful, and he's my best friend. He works hard and he loves his job. Most importantly, he makes time for us! What else could I ask for in a man? Understand that I'm happy, and I want you to be happy too. You need to stop looking for someone to pimp you around Boston like you're some type of Hollywood ho!"

Sheryl exclaims, "That's just mean! Pimp me like I'm a Hollywood ho? I don't understand."

Angie replies, "You have a good job, you're educated, you have your own, yet you're looking for a sugar daddy. These men are not going to spoil you like you may have wanted your father to spoil you. It's just not going to happen. Have you ever dealt completely with your father's death? Seriously, you may want to do that, because you are too smart to act the way you do when it comes to men. All you talk about is men spending money on you, and that's wrong. You need to start accepting these men for who they are and stop trying to groom them into the men you want them to be. You're going to run yourself crazy."

"How can you question my happiness? I have never complained or cried to you about Roland and me. I have not asked to borrow money from you. I have not shared anything negative about my relationship with Roland, but you are steady trying to prove that he's a dog. What's up? Are you jealous?"

Sheryl says, "Please. Like I said, time will soon tell all, and I'm going to be that shoulder for you to cry on."

Angie says, "I'm going to tell you this one more time. Don't say anything, just listen to me and hear me for once. Don't go and borrow somebody else's man. Get you your own steady man. What you really need is long and big. It has to be hard and trustworthy. You need a thoughtful and sincere *dick*! I keep telling you to leave those toys alone."

Sheryl says, "That sounds good. Where is he?"

Angie replies, "You're not going to get everything you want in a man. Stop trying to tell me about my man, which is something you know nothing about. Did you know that blue-collar boyfriends and husbands make up over 70 percent of our African American households? Right now you're looking for love in all the wrong places. Love is not bad once you find someone who loves you back. It should not matter if he works in the white—or blue-collar world.

"Love is not security or an image. It's an act, a verb. Love is a woman washing her man's funky underclothes. Love is unconditional. Love is spending quality time with your partner and taking care of home, as opposed to hanging out with your friends every night. It's not a game. When it's there, you know it. Love is love, Sheryl."

Sheryl says, "Calm down, Angie. You're starting to scare me."

Angie says, "I just want you to be happy, that's all. You're meeting these men with the fancy cars who are still living at home with their parents or rooming with their boys. Those men are without dreams or goals in life. Good sex is all they're offering you. Sheryl, there's no man in the world good enough to just sex me while I play house and busy mom. I'm telling you, communication with understanding and compromise are the keys to any type of relationship."

Sheryl doesn't say anything, so Angie goes on. "Take my cousin Luis, for example. He does everything for his five-year-old son, Terron. He tells his girl, Stephanie, to go out and enjoy herself while he stays at home with Terron. I can count on my fingertips the men who are involved with their children, especially on weekends when more things are happening. Stephanie is taking his kindness for weakness. Luis is far from a weak man. If Stephanie would listen to him more, be his backbone, and support him in their efforts to move forward, they would be in a better place. Instead, she just enjoys getting sexed and running the streets."

Sheryl comments, "She's just young and forgetful."

Angie replies, "Yes, she is young, but it's still not an excuse. Luis is a good man. He told me all he wanted was for Stephanie to stop running the streets and blowing money on things she didn't need. He said she has the attitude of, 'I carried our son for nine months, and now it's my prerogative to run the streets.' What she needs to do is parent Terron more and prepare herself to be the woman that she was laid down to be."

Sheryl says, "She's only twenty-four."

Angie says, "And that means what? She doesn't realize yet that good men are hard to come by. When one comes along, how does a real woman keep him? Stephanie has a lot to learn. Luis stared at me with this empty look and said, 'I could see if I was running the streets or fooling around on her. I'm confused. I'm trying to be the father that I never had.' He said he was done with her attitude and is going after sole custody. He wants to try to make it work, but I think you and Stephanie both graduated from the same school, Stupid University."

Sheryl replies, "You have mad jokes."

Angie asked, "You and Stephanie don't know each other? I'm just kidding. But Sheryl, on a serious note, you don't want to be that unhappy woman. You just don't listen to anyone. You expect things to always be your way. You have to start giving that blue-collar worker a chance."

Sheryl replies, "I can't stand you at times, but I will always love you no matter what. Thank you for taking the time to talk to me and trying to get me to see things differently."

Angie says, "You just need to balance your mind and heart. Love is a two-way street, not just one way. I'm telling you, if you keep this up, these men are going to leave you broke. As long as you allow it, a man will continue to bring you flowers, drive your Escalade, and live in your condo. Girl, I'm serious. You're too smart to be wasting time with men of no substance."

Sheryl says, "I know, but a lot of these dudes with the real good jobs are just geeks."

Angie says, "Finally, you shed some light on your choices in men. Believe me, girl, you are not in that world by yourself. A lot of the six-figure men are straight corny. I mean cornballs. That's why I love Roland—because of his swag. Working at AutoZone or not, my man accepts who he is and remembers where he came from. He has the tools needed to be a part of my team, and I love him for who he is. I already have his rib, and now I'm working on the rest of his vitals."

Sheryl replies, "You're silly."

Angie says, "Maybe so, but I'm serious. Hey, stop at Store 24 here on the left. I need to use the ATM."

Sheryl says, "Okay, cool."

Chapter 3

Store 24: A Woman's Challenge

As they walk into Store 24 in Mattapan Square, they hear that universal call: "Hey, shortyyyyy!"

Angie advises Sheryl, "Just keep walking. Do not acknowledge these fools."

Sheryl replies, "Angie, I'm a step ahead of you."

Another random guy shouts out, "Yo! Yo! I know you hear me talking to you."

Angie replies, "I'm sorry, I didn't know my mother named me Yo. Why would you address any woman if you do not know her name? I'm just trying to understand you right now. What's your name?"

Random guy says, "It's Big Mike."

Sheryl scoffs, "Big Mike!"

Random guy says, "Yeah, yeah. Big Mike."

Angie asks, "How old are you, Big Mike?" Sheryl and Angie exchange a look. Then Angie continues, "You're wearing corn rolls. You have gold fronts in your mouth, and some old, beat up, dirty white K-Swiss on your feet. You're standing in Mattapan Square in front of Store 24. For what reason? Are you waiting on the bus? Come on, Big Mike—really! Just stop while we're good. Please don't get me upset."

Big Mike repeats, "Don't get you upset? And who are you supposed to be, bitch?"

Angie says, "Oh, wait a minute. Did he just call me a bitch?"

Sheryl tells her, "Like you told me, just ignore him."

Angie replies, "I don't think so. Excuse me, what did you just call me?"

Big Mike boldly repeats, "You heard me. I called you a bitch, bitch! Acting like you're too good to holla back."

Angie says, "First of all, how dare you call me or any woman a bitch? Is your mother a bitch? Whatever she is, I know she taught you better than that. What's wrong with you saying hi or hello? I'm a bitch because I chose to ignore your ignorance? And you wonder why I ignored you!"

Big Mike replies, "I'm saying ma, let me get the number so we can hook up and get into a little som'em, som'em."

Angie replies, "A little som'em, som'em! Are you serious? Have you heard anything I just said? Sheryl, I'm feeling like DMX. 'You can't be serious.'"

Big Mike says, "Hell yeah, I'm serious. What's your number, ma? I'm feeling your sexiness."

Angie says, "Come here. Give me your ear. Are you listening?"

Big Mike replies, "I'm listening."

Angie then tells him, "You have until I come out this Store 24. If you're out here when I come out, I'm going to charge you with verbal assault on a police officer."

Big Mike, surprised, exclaims, "Oh, snap, you are one time?"

Angie replies, "Yes, I'm a cop, and I'll charge you with littering and disturbing the peace. Then I'll check you out for any priors. I hope you're not on probation, because I'd love to take the time to sit here and wait with you while a squad car comes to lock you up. You'll be in the jail being a bitch with a real Big Mike and his home boys. Now, do you want me to continue?"

Big Mike says, "No!"

Angie says, "I didn't think so. Mike, do you want me to call that officer across the street at the House of Pizza and have him detain you for harassment of a detective?"

Big Mike says again, "No!"

Angie asks, "Why are you out here harassing people? You're not in high school anymore, Mike. If you're not buying anything from this store, don't be in front of it when we come back out. Take your friends and just leave. Have a good day. You have about three minutes to be gone."

Big Mike replies, "No problem. We're out. I'm not trying to get locked back up."

Angie turns to Sheryl and asks, "This is the type of man that you're attracted to? You know what? I don't even want to know."

Sheryl says, "I don't mind fixing them up."

Angie says, "Girl, you are playing, right?"

Sheryl agrees, "Of course. I'm just messing. He was cute, though."

Angie says, "I'm not messing with you. Let me go get this money." Walking into the store, she addresses the clerk. "How are you doing, sir? Do you have an ATM in here?"

The clerk replies, "Yes. It's back by the ice machine, to the right."

Angie says, "Thank you!"

Bitter Gets Better

Sheryl shouts, "Take out an extra forty dollars for me! My purse is in the truck. I'll give it back to you later when we get to the Park Plaza."

Angie says, "That's cool." She takes out the cash and walks to the front of the store again. Sheryl is in line at the register, so Angie stands with her. "Girl, I'm telling you, Earl has the body of a Greek statue."

Sheryl says, "This line is slow, but I need this gum and stockings just in case."

Angie says, "Zeus has nothing on him. Earl is really handsome, Sheryl."

Sheryl replies, "I'll see shortly. I am excited, and feeling some type of way."

Angie urges her, "Come on, let's get out of here so I can get to my baby, Roland."

Sheryl says, "Earl's body is banging like that and he's handsome?"

Angie replies, "Earl is like that, Sheryl. Not only is he able to give you the big and stiff piece your ass needs, he's also a man of substance."

Sheryl says, "Well, you see, I'm ready to show off. Maybe I should have worn my other heels with this dress."

Angie replies, "Those shoes are nice. You're good. Don't even trip; you are good."

Sheryl says, "I know everybody there, including Roland, will be stuck in the twilight zone when I walk in the hotel lobby. I'm ready to party."

Angie replies, "Everyone including Roland? I know you're tripping now."

Sheryl says, "Your body is cute, but not as cute as mine. Girl, I said that in chapter one."

Angie says, "I know. I was there when you wrote it. Yes, your body is cute; however, I'm the complete package."

Finally, it is Sheryl's turn to hand her purchases to the cashier. Angie exclaims, "About time! Girl, pay for your things so we can go."

Sheryl asks with a concerned look, "Do you think Big Mike and his boys are going to be outside?"

Angie says, "I'm not thinking about that fool. He is not about to mess up my night. Good night, sir."

The cashier responds, "Good night."

Angie says to Sheryl, "Come on, let's go."

Sheryl says, "There go Big Mike and his friends down the street."

Angie says, "Good."

Sheryl muses, "He was kind of cute."

Angie says, "See what I mean? I'm not messing with you. Your butt is just crazy."

As they arrive at the Park Plaza Hotel, they search for a place to park. Angie tells Sheryl, "Park in the garage across the street."

Sheryl says, "I'm not parking in that garage. They're asking twenty dollars for four hours."

Angie says, "Twenty dollars! I know that's not right. You can park at a meter for free all night."

Sheryl replies, "I know, right?"

Angie says, "That blue truck is pulling out on the left."

Sheryl says, "Good. It's close to the hotel too. Good timing. I hope Earl is on point."

Angie says, "Like I told you, his body is worth a couple of late-night booty calls."

Sheryl replies, "I hear you. So, Angie, have you thought about dipping in it yourself?"

Angie asks, "Dip in what?"

Sheryl answers, "You know—with Earl."

Angie says, "I would never. Sheryl, we're not having this conversation. For the record, I will never cheat on Roland. He's all I want and need. It's not worth it in the end."

Sheryl says, "Maybe not, but you keep thinking about Earl."

Angie says, "Are you serious, Sheryl? I'm not thinking about that man. I just made a comment or two about his fine body. Girl, hurry up and park this truck so I can see my man before I hurt you. I told you what's wrong with you."

Sheryl replies, "I'm just checking."

Sheryl and Angie enter the hotel lobby. Sheryl immediately observes, "There are some fine men in here."

Angie says, "There's my baby, over by the window."

Sheryl asks, "Which one of those fine brothers is Earl?"

Angie replies, "I don't know, but come on. Any of them will do for you."

Sheryl says, "I see you still have jokes."

Angie says to Roland, "Hi, baby!"

Roland says, "Hey, sweetie! You guys just got here?"

Angie replies, "Yes."

Roland says, "What's up, Sheryl?"

Sheryl says, "Hello."

Roland tells Sheryl, "You look nice."

Sheryl answers, "Yes, I know. Thank you!"

Roland says, "Oh, Earl will be right back. These are coworkers of mine: Wayne, John, Dave, and Sean. This is my girl Angie and her girl Sheryl."

The coworkers respond, "What's up, ladies?"

Angie and Sheryl reply, "Hi, guys."

Roland says, "Here's Earl now. Sheryl, this is my boy Earl, and Earl, this is Sheryl."

Earl greets her, "How are you doing, Sheryl? It's nice to finally meet you."

Sheryl replies, "Likewise, Earl. You are very handsome."

Earl says, "Thanks! This white rose is for you."

Sheryl asks, "And what is the meaning of a white rose? It smells nice."

Earl tells her, "It stands for friendship."

Sheryl replies, "Oh, we're friends now? I'm kidding; just giving you a hard time. This is nice. How sweet! Thank you."

Angie says, "Sheryl, while you and Earl get to know each other, Roland and I will be over at the table."

Sheryl says, "Okay. We'll see you shortly. Earl and I will check out this waterfall. You know, and chat a little bit."

Angie replies, "That's cool. You guys do that."

As they look at the waterfall, Sheryl says, "Thanks again for my rose, Earl. Are you always this thoughtful, or are you trying to get some brownie points?"

Earl says, "Actually both. I'm feeling you."

Sheryl asks, "What are you feeling about me?"

Earl replies, "Well, you are very attractive. Why are you single?"

Sheryl says, "How do you know I'm single?"

Earl says, "I know a happily involved woman will not be out with another man, for starters."

Sheryl admits, "Okay, you got me. It's by choice. I'm just investing in me at the moment. Plus, I have not met the right guy yet. I would like to be involved, but I'm waiting for a good man to surface. Until then, I'm just doing me."

Earl says, "And you're doing a very good job at it."

Sheryl asks, "So tell me: are you a good man?"

Earl replies, "I like to think that I'm a good man."

Sheryl says, "Why are you staring at me like that?"

Earl says, "I'm sorry for staring, but your dress is nice. You look good, girl!"

Sheryl replies, "Thank you!"

Earl asks, "Are you from Boston?"

Sheryl replies, "No; I'm from California."

Earl says, "California? I have some friends out west. What part of California are you from?"

Sheryl says, "I'm from South Central."

Earl says, "I went there last year. California has some nice homes. It's hard to stomach that gang-banging is so popular coming out of such a beautiful place."

Sheryl says, "Well, it's there, believe me."

Earl says, "I know. These days we have crime everywhere. It's in our inner cities and suburbs."

Sheryl asks, "Why is a sexy man like yourself single? Where's your girlfriend?"

Earl replies, "Girlfriend? You mean my wife of four and a half years. She's at home."

Surprised, Sheryl demands, "Earl, you're married?"

Earl says, "Yes, but it's cool."

Sheryl says, "It's cool? No, it's not cool. That's so disrespectful. Why are you here with me if you have a wife at home? You know what? I don't even want to know. I've done nothing but prepare to meet you with intentions to hook up. Out of all the men in Boston, I had to meet you—a man who's having problems at home. I'm leaving."

Sheryl throws the rose at Earl and says, "'Friend'? Yeah, right! You're not worth the breath! I bet you told your wife that you were hanging out with your boys, right?"

Sheryl walks away to find Angie. She finds her with Roland and says, "Roland, are you taking Angie home? Because I'm out of here."

Roland replies, "Of course. What's up, Sheryl? You good?"

Sheryl snaps, "No, I am not!"

Angie asks, "Girl, what happened?"

Sheryl replies, "Earl is married! This man has a wife at home, and he's out on a date with me! Roland, you knew he had a wife? Did you think I got down like that?"

Angie says, "Sheryl, calm down. Talk to me."

Sheryl tells her, "I'm straight. I'm just going to go home before I lose it. I would rather be at home doing some work than be here with this man."

Angie says, "Don't leave."

Sheryl replies, "Girl, I'm going home. Call me if Roland starts tripping."

Earl comes up and says, "Yo, Roland, why is your girl leaving?"

Sheryl says, "Whatever, man. My name is Sheryl, thank you. If your wife were here, you wouldn't be mad, now, would you? You are sad. I'll see you later, Angie."

As Sheryl walks gracefully to the elevator, Angie says, "Sheryl, hold up. I'm coming with you."

Sheryl responds, "Stay here with your man, girl. I'll be all right."

Angie says, "Well, at least I can walk you to your truck."

Sheryl says, "Cool. Come on."

Angie says, "Roland, I'll be back. I'm going to walk Sheryl to her truck."

Roland says, "I'll be the sexiest man in black at the bar."

Angie tells him, "Roland, you're so silly. I'll be back, boy."

Roland asks Earl, "What the hell happened?"

Earl replies, "Man, all was good until she asked me if I was single."

Roland says, "Well, what did you tell her?"

Earl says, "I was telling her the truth, but before I could finish saying anything, she started going crazy. Man, she flipped!"

Roland replies, "You think?"

Earl says, "Man, I'm going to give her about twenty minutes to leave. Then I'm going home to work on things with my wife. Don't try to hook me up ever again. I'm out."

Roland says, "You might as well stay now."

Earl replies, "Nah. I'm missing my wife now. We have problems, but she is far from a crazy. I'm keeping my marriage."

Roland says, "I hear you, man. It's cheaper to keep her."

While waiting for the elevator, Angie says, "What's up? What happened?"

Sheryl replies, "The man has a wife. Girl, he's sexy and a little charming, but he is not all that. I wonder if I was supposed to be okay with the fact that this dude has a wife at home?"

Angie says, "That's exactly what we were talking about on the way here—unhappy situations. Earl is simply not happy at home. I'm telling you Sheryl, love is no joke. Don't get married for the wrong reasons. You'll be that lonely wife at home. You might as well just stay and mingle because there's nothing to do at home."

Sheryl says, "I'm good. He made me hate all men tonight. Just like R. Kelly said, 'One man can make one woman hate all men.'"

Angie replies, "Girl, I know that's right."

Sheryl says, "I wish this elevator would hurry up and come."

Angie says, "Here it is."

Sheryl complains, "I can never meet someone worth meeting. I'm tired of being lonely and coming home to an empty house."

Angie says, "Wait a minute. Are you crying? Let me get my bag; I'm coming home with you."

Sheryl says, "Nah, I'm straight."

Angie says, "You sure?"

Sheryl says, "Really. I'm okay."

Angie says, "Here's some tissue. Wipe your tears, girl. Don't let no man get you depressed to the point you're crying. You don't even know this man."

Sheryl replies, "I'm just tired, Angie. I envy what you and Roland have."

Angie says, "You envy the relationship Roland and I have? It takes a lot of work to maintain what we have. It's not easy."

Sheryl says, "True, and I still think he's a dog. He's going to bite one day. Mark my words, girl. Mark my words. I'm sorry if I messed up your night."

Angie replies, "My night is just beginning. We'll talk about it later."

Sheryl says, "You hold on to Roland, because there's nothing out here but a bunch of mutts. These men will try to sex everything with a wet or dry hole. Men are not worthy of being called dogs. Mutt is a better name for the men that I have experienced. Calling them dogs is giving them too much credit."

Angie asks, "Are you going to be okay?"

Sheryl replies, "Yes. I'm good."

Angie says, "Okay, girl. Give me a hug."

Sheryl says, "I'll see you in the morning. I'm about to get me my Chinese food, run me a bubble bath, and maybe watch a movie."

Angie says, "Cool. Call me when you get in, okay?"

Sheryl says, "Will do. Good night."

Angie replies, "Good night, and be careful driving home."

Sheryl gets in her SUV and pulls out, thinking, "I don't believe this. What movies do I have at home? I didn't even eat. I hope the Red Dragon in Mattapan is still open. It should be; it's still early."

As Sheryl pulls up to the restaurant and finds parking, she thinks, "Who's this fine brother I see through the window? Let me freshen up. I wonder if he'll come back to the house with me? If he has a wife, shit, she can watch. Listen to me. Let me stop talking crazy. He is fine, though."

Sheryl enters the restaurant and walks directly to him, saying, "Excuse me, have you ordered yet?"

The man says, "Yes, I'm all set."

Sheryl thinks, "Okay, he has a nice smile and all of his teeth. That's a good start. He's easy to look at. Why not? I have nothing else to do tonight."

Then Sheryl speaks to the guy behind the register. "Hello. How are you, sir?"

The cashier replies, "Hi. What are you ordering?"

Sheryl says, "Can I have your mixed vegetables over house rice, and sweet and sour chicken?"

The cashier says, "Sure. Would you like anything to drink with that?"

Sheryl replies, "Yes; let me have a Coke."

The cashier tells her, "That will be $12.49."

Sheryl says, "Here you go, sir. About how long?"

The cashier says, "It will be ready in about ten minutes."

Sheryl replies, "Thanks."

The man she noticed from her SUV introduces himself. "How are you doing? I'm Chris."

Sheryl says, "Hi, Chris. I'm Sheryl. What time do you have?"

Chris replies, "It's nine forty-five. Are you running late to meet your man?"

Sheryl laughs. "My man! Umm, no. I'm just coming back from a date that did not go well."

Chris asks, "Are you okay?"

Sheryl says, "Yes. I'm fine now. Thanks for asking."

Chris continues, "What did he do? Why are you laughing?"

Sheryl replies, "I don't know why I thought I was going to have a good night. All the men I meet turn out to be jerks."

Chris says, "Well, I'm about to sit down to eat. Would you like to join me? I'm a good listener."

Sheryl says, "Chris, you don't understand."

Chris says, "Well, like I said, I'm a good listener. I've got some time. I just came out to grab some last minute items for a little get-together I'm having tomorrow."

Sheryl asks, "Are, you married?"

Chris answers, "Yes, for a year now."

Sheryl asks, "Are you happy?"

Chris declares, "I wouldn't trade it for the world. I'm blessed."

Sheryl replies, "Wow, that's great. Do you have any children?"

Chris says, "No. I have no children."

Sheryl says, "What type of get-together are you having tomorrow?"

Chris says, "Nothing big. A couple of friends and family members just hanging out. You and a friend are more than welcome to come by and have some drinks, eat, hang out, and chill with us."

The cashier says to Sheryl, "Hello! Your food is ready now."

Sheryl says to Chris, "Excuse me. I have to go get that."

Chris says, "I'll get it for you."

Sheryl says, "Thank you! Can I have some more napkins and duck sauce, please?"

The cashier says, "That's an extra twenty-five cents for the duck sauce."

Chris gives a soft chuckle and walks to the eating tables. Sheryl says, "Your food smells good."

Chris replies, "Oh, it's very good. My partner and I eat here often. About three times a week. So tell me, Sheryl, what's going on with you?"

Sheryl tells him, "I don't feel too comfortable talking to you about what's going on with me. I don't know you."

Chris acknowledges, "I respect that. Well, tell me about your long and interesting day."

Sheryl thinks, "What the hell?" Out loud, she says, "I'm just tired of meeting sorry men."

Chris says, "Now that's a topic worth listening to."

Sheryl says, "I'm starting to think that I was put on this earth to work. All my relationships to date have failed. I keep finding sorry men."

Chris says, "Finding men? You shouldn't be searching for a man. You have to just let that happen. All relationships are gambles, whether they are intimate, work-related, or sports-affiliated."

Sheryl says, "You sound like my girl Angie."

Chris asks, "Is that a bad thing?"

Sheryl replies, "It's actually a good thing. I love her to death."

Chris says, "Cool."

Sheryl says, "You just took me there for a minute."

Chris says, "Well, building trust is very hard. As we meet people, we have to believe in them until they give us reason not to trust them. When they do that, we have to make the decision to stay or to move on. The sad thing is that most people choose to stay in a bad situation, thinking things will get better."

Sheryl says, "I know that's right. But I just have bad luck, Chris. It never fails for me. I always meet the sorry men."

Chris says, "I'm not a sorry man."

Sheryl responds, "Maybe, maybe not, but you're married, and I don't date guys who are married! I don't believe I'm about to tell you my business when I don't even know you."

Chris says, "Most people will talk to strangers about their business before they chat with someone they know."

Sheryl asks, "Why is that?"

Chris replies, "Some say it's because a stranger will give an unbiased opinion."

Sheryl says, "Okay. I never thought about it that way. It does make sense. Anyway, here goes . . .

"I met this guy tonight who I thought would be cool because he was my girl's boyfriend's boy. When I first saw this man, I was, like, this is going to be a good night. He was good-looking. He had nice eyes, a nice build, and a strong body. He was well groomed. I mean, he really presented himself nice. He gave me a warm hug and a white rose."

Chris comments, "Oh, he had some romance with him."

Sheryl replies, "Yes, some romance. That's what I'm saying. The white rose had me lost in the moment. This man had me right from the start. Chris, why was he married?"

With a surprised look, Chris says, "Stop playing. He was married?"

Sheryl says, "Yes, I kid you not. He was telling me that everything was okay. Talking about it's cool. Chris, I'm not trying to break up anyone's happy home. I'm just trying to build my own. I'm tired of this whole dating scene."

Chris replies, "I hear you. I hated dating, myself."

Sheryl says, "I need to go through my little black Gucci book and spark up an old flame."

Chris says again, "I hear you. Well, at my get-together tomorrow, there will be a lot of single men floating around. Come out and be social. Are you the social type?"

Sheryl says, "I get along good with people."

Chris replies, "Good. Bring some business cards with you, so you can do some networking. Enjoy yourself. Come through around three o'clock, if you decide to come."

Sheryl says, "Let me think about it. I'll call you tomorrow."

Chris says, "Here's my address and number. I hope to hear from you."

Sheryl replies, "You might just see me. Thanks for the ear. I do feel a little better."

Chris says, "No problem. That's my phone ringing. Duty calls."

Sheryl says, "Okay, thanks. I'll call you. You have a good night!"

Chris replies, "You too. Good night!"

Chris walks out of the Dragon and smiles as he catches her looking at his butt. He simply waves good-bye. Sheryl heads home. She calls Angie and says, "Hey, what's up? How did the rest of your night go?"

Angie says, "Girl, Roland and Earl started arguing. Roland said that he thought that Earl and his wife were on bad terms, and his wife had moved out of the house. That was what Earl told him the last time they talked, a month ago. Roland says he's sorry, he didn't know that Earl was back at home with his wife."

Sheryl says, "Girl, I'm not tripping off that. Tell him it's cool."

Angie says, "I thought about you all night. Especially while Roland and Earl was arguing. When they went downstairs, I was going to leave then, but when I called, your phone just rang. Are you just getting in?"

Sheryl says, "Yeah. I met this guy at the Dragon!"

Angie says, "Well, was he cute?"

Sheryl says, "He was okay, but he's married. At least he was up front about it."

Angie groans. "Here we go."

Sheryl says, "Nah. He was cool. We spoke a little bit, and he invited us to a get-together he's having tomorrow at his house."

Angie says, "Us!"

Sheryl answers, "Yes, us! You're not doing anything tomorrow but painting your toenails."

Angie says, "True."

Sheryl says, "Good. He told me to bring some business cards for networking."

Angie hedges, "I don't know . . ." Hey, since last night got a little crazy we ended up sailing the room at the Park Plaza last night to some friends of Roland. I'll give you your half of the money for the suite in the morning.

Sheryl says, "That's cool, girl, just come by in the morning. We'll cook breakfast and leave from here. Come over around ten."

Angie gives in. "All right! I'll see you in the morning, girl. What are you going to do now?"

Sheryl replies, "I'm about to soak in some warm water and Epsom salts."

Angie says, "I hear that. I'll see you tomorrow. Good night."

Sheryl says, "Night."

Sheryl hangs up the phone and thinks, "While my bath water is running, let me grab all my little knickknacks for a relaxing soak. I have my cherry-scented candles, my movies, some white wine, and a bowl of cherries and white grapes. I'll light my candles, place them around my spa bath, and relax.

"I love the smell of these candles. Time for a good, old-school movie. Let's see, I have *The Player's Club*, *How To Be a Player*, *The Hurricane*, *Big Daddy*, *Brown Sugar*, *Honey*, *The Last Man Standing*, and *How Stella Got Her Groove Back*. I wish somebody would tell me how to get a groove. I'm not in the mood for any of these.

"I haven't seen this in a while. *Nine-Inch Wonder*! It's that porn I took from Angie before she met Roland. This is cool. I'll watch this for a bit.

"Yeah, this will work. *Nine-Inch Wonder*. Whoa! Boy, you're about to hurt that girl. I see why they call you Nine-Inch Wonder.

"My water is just a little too hot. Some cool water should make it just right. Let me pause this for a minute while I get this water right.

"Ahhh, much better. These jets feel so good on my body. Ummm. No need to rewind, I like this scene right here. Boy, slow down; she can't handle all that! Just look at you handle your business. Like an oil-well pump. Thrust after thrust after thrust.

"If I were playing that role, Mr. Nine-Inch Wonder, it would be like the WWF, because I'd have you tapped out in the first round. Let me put this wine down, close my eyes, and take my overdue journey. Then I'll get in my bed."

Chapter 4

Mistaken Identity

Sheryl wakes up to the phone ringing at nine thirty. She answers, "Good morning."

Angie replies, "What's up, girl?"

Sheryl says, "Nothing. Just getting up. Your call startled me a little bit."

Angie says, "I'm sorry. I thought you were up already."

Sheryl says, "Girl, I threw in *Nine-Inch Wonder* and fell straight to sleep afterward. I got in my bed and was out until your call just now."

Angie asks, "You still have my DVD?"

Sheryl says, "Yes. I watched it last night while I was soaking."

Angie says, "Anyway, I got a taste for some French toast, scrambled eggs hard with cheese, beef patties, and a glass of fresh-squeezed orange juice."

Sheryl says, "Just bring me the eggs, girl."

Angie asks, "What's wrong with you? You have company? Who came over last night? Don't tell me that guy from the Dragon."

Sheryl answers, "Girl, I just told you. I watched *Nine-Inch Wonder*, and that dude put me to sleep just watching him."

Angie laughs and says, "I know what you mean. I know exactly what you mean. Ummm, can I get my movie back?"

Sheryl says, "Oh, you still want that?"

Angie says, "I do."

Sheryl inquires, "What time are you leaving to come through?"

Angie says, "We said ten yesterday, but sounds like that's too early. I'll leave in about an hour."

Sheryl replies, "That's cool. That will give me time to clean my house."

Angie says, "All right. I'll see you shortly."

Sheryl says, "I'll leave the door open for you. Just come in."

Angie says, "Okay. I'll see you in a few."

At eleven forty-five, Sheryl's doorbell rings. She calls out, "The door is open; come in! I'll be out in one second. I'm just cleaning my bathroom. I have cherries, grapes, and spilled wine on the floor. Girl, I had a moment last night. I'll be right out. You can start cooking if you like."

To Sheryl's surprise, she has invited strangers into her home. They softly shout, "Hello? Hello!"

Sheryl comes out of the bathroom and says, "Whoa, I'm sorry. Can you get out of my house? Who are you? Why are you here?"

One of the strangers says, "Hi. My name is Michael Heart, and this is Sister Carol Stevenson. We didn't mean to startle you, but you said come in, and I assumed you were speaking to us."

Sheryl replies, "No, I was not. I'm expecting a friend."

Brother Michael says, "Well, since we're here, may we speak with you? We're Jehovah's Witnesses."

Sheryl says, "I can see who you are now, but I thought you were my friend. I'm not interested."

Brother Michael urges her, "We won't be long. We would like to invite you to one of our studies."

Sheryl says, "No, thank you. I'm a born-again Christian."

Brother Michael says, "I'll leave you a *Watch Tower* to read at your leisure."

Sheryl insists, "No, I'm good. I'm a Christian. You guys enjoy your day and take care."

As Michael and Carol are walking out, Angie walks in to Sheryl's condo. With a strange look, Angie asks, "Hey, who was that?"

Sheryl replies, "Some Jehovah's Witnesses I thought were you."

Angie shouts, "You thought were me? How did you think that?"

Sheryl says, "I was in my bathroom and heard a knock. I screamed out that the door was open and to come in. To my surprise, there's strangers in my living room! What's up, girl?"

Angie answers, "Nothing. I'm glad your kitchen is clean because I'm ready to eat. I hope you have everything we need. I brought some T-bone steaks to go along with the eggs and French toast. What do you have to drink? Damn, I forgot the drinks."

Sheryl says, "Look in the bottom cabinet on the bottom shelf. You'll find juices there. Do me a favor and put the cherry and grape juices in the freezer."

Angie asks, "You don't have any wine, girl?"

Sheryl tells her, "You are not in Europe. It's too early to be drinking some damn wine."

Angie says, "I'm trying to stay young like the Europeans."

Sheryl says, "I think you need to lead the whole lifestyle, not just get drunk off wine. Girl, you're crazy. No, I don't have any wine."

Angie asks, "So what's the plan for the day?"

Sheryl says, "Eat and relax until it's time to leave."

Angie replies, "Sounds like a plan to me. I'm going to do my toes while we chill."

Sheryl says, "You can do mine as well."

Angie jokes, "You need a professional and a miracle to do your toes."

Sheryl says, "We have jokes, I see."

Angie says seriously, "So what's up with this Chris guy? He's married?"

Sheryl says, "Yes, and why are all the good men taken?"

Angie replies, "There's truth in what you say, but you have to slow down and stop chasing the wrong men. I tell you, you're too damn materialistic. Stop looking for benefits and get with the substance. You have your own benefits and good ones at that. Find you a hardworking man who respects you. I bet you'll be much happier."

Sheryl says, "Girl, anyway, I'm hungry. I'm not trying to hear that soapbox. I am trying to eat."

Angie asks, "Do you have A. 1. steak sauce?"

Sheryl says, "I do. Look on the top shelf. I can't recall the last time I made French toast for myself. My house smells like back in the day, on Sundays after church."

Angie says, "What do you mean?"

Sheryl says, "Either this food is that good, or I'm just hungry."

Angie replies, "It's both. I saw your food from last night in the refrigerator. You hardly touched it. And my food is simply good."

Sheryl says, "I didn't know you had skills like this, Angie. From this point, dinners are at your place, and you're cooking."

Angie says, "See, you just need a man."

Sheryl exclaims, "Whatever! I'm just saying."

Angie comments from out of the blue, "Girl, Roland must have taken a blue pill last night."

Sheryl says, "Why do you say that?"

Angie replies, "My baby was overly aggressive, but I liked it. He brought the animal out in me last night. He put it down. My pussy is sore. Do you have some sandwich bags?"

Sheryl repeats, "Sandwich bags?"

Angie says, "Yes, so I can put some ice on my girl. Quit asking me questions and just hand me a sandwich bag and some ice."

Sheryl says, "Look on the top of the fridge. What's up with the ice? I've heard of ice for stimulation, but what are you using it for?"

Angie replies, "My girl is bruised and swollen. The ice takes the inflammation down."

Sheryl asks, "Roland put it down like that?"

With a huge smile on her face, Angie confirms, "Always!"

Sheryl says, "It must be nice."

Angie says, "Girl, anyway, is the movie *Soul Food* in the case?"

Sheryl says, "No. It's on the top rack of the closet. You're really using that ice?"

Angie replies, "Yes! I am sore! I can't sit down without twitching."

Sheryl says, "I'm sore myself."

Angie, surprised, says, "What are you sore from?"

Sheryl states, "I think I gave myself circular finger burn."

Angie laughs. "Circular finger burn! Girl, you are just crazy. I have never heard of anything like that. Really!"

Sheryl replies, "For real, my girl is tingling a little bit."

Angie tells her, "I'm through with you. You're funny, Sheryl, but that dude who plays Nine-Inch Wonder is a stud."

Sheryl says, "That man had me in dream land."

Angie says, "Let's eat, relax, paint the toenails while watching this movie, go wash your truck, andthen go by Chris's house. I also have a taste for some ice cream."

Sheryl agrees, "Yes! Some ice cream would be good."

Angie replies, "Cool. Then that's the plan."

About three hours later (2:50 p.m.), they leave Sheryl's place to wash the truck and head to Chris's place.. Sheryl asks, "Angie, where do you go to get your car washed?"

Angie says, "I normally go over by South Bay."

Sheryl makes a face. "Ewwww, it's always packed over there."

Angie says, "Where do you go?"

Sheryl replies, "I go to the Scrub-A-Dub & Wax on American Legion Highway. Plus, they got that ice cream shop across the street."

Angie repeats excitedly, "Ice cream shop?"

Sheryl says, "Yes! They have some good ice cream too, girl. I do have a taste for some sherbet."

Angie says, "Sherbet? I want me a banana split with nuts, whipped cream, fudge, caramel, and two cherries."

Sheryl says, "Now, that sounds good too. I may have to hold off on the sherbet. Yeah, a banana split will work."

Angie replies, "Let's get the truck washed first."

As they pull in to the car wash, Sheryl says, "Do you see the brother in the BMW to the left vacuuming his car?"

Angie says, "He's ugly. He has no teeth in his mouth and his dreads are tired. Are you serious? Sheryl, your butt is backward. Look at the guy, not the car."

Sheryl exclaims, "Oh, hell, nah! He is ugly. What was I looking at?"

Angie says, "Exactly! Now, look at the dude coming out of the waiting room. He seems professional with a little thug in him, and he has a nice truck."

Sheryl says, "His truck is smaller than mine."

Angie says, "Mr. BMW's hair was longer than yours, but that didn't stop your interest."

Sheryl says, "His car is banging and I wanted to drive it for a brief moment. I think I want one."

Angie says, "That dude was skinny and short, plus ugly. He looked sick."

Sheryl replies, "Oh, Angie, you're wrong for that."

Angie says, "Look at him. Wait a minute, wait a minute! Where are the four little crumb-snatchers going? Oh, could he be a daddy?"

Sheryl grumbles, "Whatever, Angie!"

Angie says, "Pretty boys are good for making babies and being late for dates because they're trying to look better than the women. Now, take a real close look at this guy. He's looking like a sportswear model in his cute truck. He's about six feet, with a nice, strong, athletic body, nice clothes, and a tight fade and a trim."

Sheryl says, "Yeah, he's cute, but damn, his truck is small."

Angie asks, "What's the deal with the truck being small? Who cares? That's good eye candy. The kind you have to cut a sister for showing her butt trying to seek the attention of your man.

"You better stop being so materialistic, Sheryl. You have everything you want. I don't understand why you're so lost. You make me sick sometimes with this gold-digger attitude. Girl, tell the man what type of wash you want."

Sheryl says to the cashier, "Oh, how are you doing, sir?"

The cashier replies, "How are you? What wash can I get for you?"

Sheryl asks, "Can I have the works with the tire shine and new car spray, please?"

The cashier replies, "That's twenty-two fifty."

Sheryl says, "Here you go, and thank you."

The cashier says, "Are you guys staying in the car? If so, put the car in neutral and exit to the right when the sign reads 'exit now.'"

Angie says, "Sheryl, you sound like a dude asking for a car wash."

Sheryl says, "I got that from Brian."

Angie says, "Brian! You mean Brian from school?"

Sheryl replies, "Yes! Every time we went through a car wash, he would be, like, 'Yo, hit me up with the works package with the tire shine and new car air freshener.'"

Angie asks, "How's he doing?"

Sheryl says, "The last I heard from him, he was in the NFL playing with the Raiders, married, with three little boys."

Angie says, "He's married?"

Sheryl replies, "For two years now."

Angie says, "Good for him. Who did he marry?"

Sheryl says, "I don't know. I think he married some girl name Tasha Brown from California. She attended Cal State. He met her while supposedly studying for a final they had the following day."

Angie laughs and says, "Let me find out you're a long-distance stalker. I thought you didn't know, Sheryl."

Sheryl says, "Well, that's all I know."

Angie replies, "Your butt is crazy."

The truck moves through the car wash. Angie observes, "This is kind of cool. I've never been through a car wash before. I always walk on the side, watching for the lights for the type of wash I got to light up as the car rolls through."

Sheryl says, "I always roll through the car wash. These people like to steal stuff out of your car. Maybe that's what happened to some of my CDs."

Angie says, "Hey, the man is telling you to pull over there. Why over there? Is this where they do the tire shine? I never put tire shine on my tires when I get my car washed. So that's the reason why I be seeing tires shining?"

Sheryl says with exasperation, "Angie."

Angie replies, "I'm not kidding. I thought it was a type of tire everyone was buying."

Sheryl says, "Don't worry. I got you, girl. I'll put you up on the game."

Angie says, "Let's go get that banana split."

Sheryl says, "It's packed."

Angie says, "Oh, snap, there's Trigga."

Sheryl asks, "Who is Trigga? Why are you sliding down in your seat?"

Angie says, "Damn, I don't want him to see me like this."

Sheryl says, "Like what?"

Angie replies, "Girl, Trigga went through the academy with me."

Sheryl says, "Oh, the one-night stand you had before you and Roland became serious?"

Angie says, "Yes! I get weak when I'm around him."

Sheryl says, "What? You mean *Angie* has a crush on another man?"

Angie replies, "No. I don't have a crush on him. It's just hard for me to say no to him."

Sheryl says, "I don't believe what I'm hearing from you."

Angie says, "It's not what you think. We always show up in the same places. I feel guilty around him."

Sheryl says, "Why do you feel guilty around him when you are so in love with Roland?"

Angie explains, "Roland got in because Trigga had field training for three months. During that time, Roland and I got together. Then I decided Roland was who I wanted."

Sheryl says, "So you never told Trigga the deal with Roland?"

Angie says, "I told him about Roland, and he wished us happiness."

Sheryl says, "Whatever, girl! You know that was not sincere."

Angie continues, "He's actually seeing one of our coworkers. He introduced Roland and I one time when we saw them at Legal Sea Foods. I was nervous, because the last time I'd seen Trigga was that weekend before he went off to field training."

Sheryl says, "Yes! The night of the first one-night stand."

Angie says, "I have not seen that fine man since, but I'm happy for him."

Sheryl asks, "Are you sure Roland is the one?"

Angie replies, "Oh, I'm positive about my baby Roland. I just hate that I didn't bring closure like I should have back then."

Sheryl says, "Well, there's no time like the present."

Angie looks at Sheryl and says, "You are right! I'm going to end the inner feeling I have about this man right now."

Sheryl says, "Go ahead, girl. I got your back. I'll order the splits. How do you want yours?"

Angie replies, "Order mine with strawberry and vanilla ice cream, nuts, caramel, the hot fudge, the whipped cream, and two cherries. Thanks, girl."

Sheryl says, "No problem. Just handle your business."

As Sheryl parks the truck, eye eye contact is made between Angie and Trigga. Trigga walks over to the truck and speaks. "Angie, what's up? How's everything? It's been a while."

Angie replies, "It has. It's been about six months. How's the life of a field agent?"

Trigga says, "I like it. It's time-consuming, but I love the work. How's work for you?"

Angie says, "About the same, time-consuming, but I love it as well. You're still looking good, Trigga."

Trigga replies, "Thanks! You're looking very nice as well."

Angie asks, "So, how's your girl?"

Trigga says, "We're not together anymore. The job meant I couldn't provide the time she demanded."

Angie says, "I'm sorry to hear that. When did you guys break up?"

Trigga says, "It's been about four months now."

Bitter Gets Better

Angie tells him, "Roland and I are doing well. We are happy."

Trigga says, "You and Roland are still together? I'm surprised. I actually thought you and I were going to try to see if something was there."

Angie replies, "As I said, we are happy. Trigga, I'm going to be frank with you because of how we stopped talking. I was feeling you at that time. I thought you were handsome, smart, career-minded, and funny. When you left, I knew you had to focus on career, so I did not call. That's when Roland and I progressed."

Trigga says, "I feel you and respect your shared words. I'm happy for you guys. Why are you laughing?"

Angie says, "My girl Sheryl thought you were just talking when you said you were happy for Roland and me."

Trigga exclaims, "Really! She played me like that?"

Angie says, "Pay my girl no mind. She's just looking out for me. But you are looking good. You're smart, you have a great career, you're single with no children. Some woman is going to be lucky to hook you."

Trigga says, "Nah. At the moment I have to finish getting settled in my career. I'm not where I want to be. Maybe within a year or two, I'll be ready to give that one hundred percent."

Angie says, "That's fair of you. At least you have a plan. Hey, here's my girl now. Sheryl, this is my friend Trigga. Trigga, this is Sheryl."

Trigga greets her, "How are you, Sheryl?"

Sheryl replies, "Hi, Trigga, how are you?"

Trigga says, "I'm good. Just maintaining and trying to live right."

Sheryl says, "I know that's right."

Angie butts in and says, "Well, it was nice seeing you, Trigga."

Sheryl adds, "Yes, it was nice meeting you. Take care."

Sheryl and Angie sits in the truck, and eat their ice cream. Then they head out to the get-together at Chris's place. Sheryl asks, "How did it go with Trigga?"

Angie replies, "Well, he's no longer with his coworker, and he wanted to see if we could get something started."

Sheryl says, "What? What did you say?"

Angie says, "I told him the truth. Roland and I are happy. I also told him that you thought he was full of mess because of the best wishes he told me for my relationship with Roland."

Sheryl says, "Why did you tell him that?"

Angie replies, "He did not trip. I think he was surprised that me and Roland are still together. That was it, really. I told him that my relationship was serious with Roland, and he wished us the best again."

Sheryl asks, "Did he ask for your number?"

Angie says, "No. Even if he asked for it, I would not have given it to him. I'm not disrespecting Roland."

Sheryl says, "It's something about Roland. He seems to be too perfect."

Angie gives Sheryl a stern look. Sheryl answers it with, "I know, and I'm keeping my mouth shut until he gives you a reason. You got that."

Angie says, "Enough about me. Tell me about Chris."

Sheryl says, "There's nothing to say about him other than he's married and he seems cool."

Angie asks, "Was he flirting with you last night?"

Sheryl replies, "Nah. He was just listening and talking to me."

Angie exclaims, "Talking to you!"

Sheryl says, "Yes; we spoke about what happened at the hotel."

Angie says, "You told him that?"

Sheryl explains, "I needed to vent, and I wanted you to stay and enjoy your night. I might be crazy, but you know I don't hate on my worse enemy. We spoke about that and just had small, random conversation. It was cool."

Angie says, "Well, let's go by Chris's spot now and just chill."

Sheryl says, "Yeah. I want to see what his wife looks like."

Angie warns, "You better leave that man alone."

Sheryl replies, "I just want to see what his wife looks like. You know, I want to see his taste in women. Hey, his number should be on that Dragon menu on the backseat. Grab it for me, please?"

Angie says, "You are too much. Here it is."

Sheryl says, "I hope he answers the phone."

The phone rings, and Chris answers, "Hello!"

Sheryl says, "Chris, this is Sheryl."

Chris replies, "What's up, Sheryl?"

Sheryl says, "Hi! How are you doing?"

Chris says, "I'm straight. Are you coming through?"

Sheryl replies, "Yeah, that's why I was calling you. My girl and I are en route."

Chris says, "Oh, okay. Well, as soon as you make the left onto my street, it's number 4201—the fifth house on the right side. Find a parking spot and head straight to the backyard."

Sheryl asks, "Do you need us to bring anything?"

Chris says, "Just bring yourselves and an empty stomach."

Sheryl says, "Okay. We'll see you soon. Bye for now."

Chris replies, "I'll see you shortly."

Sheryl asks Angie, "What street did that sign say?"

Angie answers, "Dartmouth. He's over by the Copley Mall. He must stay in those brownstones over there."

Sheryl says, "Girl, he's paid."

Angie says, "This is the street right here. His address is 4201."

Sheryl says, "Look at all these nice cars!"

Angie tells Sheryl to hold on and says to a stranger, "Excuse me, does Chris stay here?"

The stranger says, "Yeah. I'm talking to him now on the phone. What's your name?"

Sheryl says, "Tell him it's Sheryl."

The stranger says, "Actually, you can park right here because I'm leaving."

Angie asks, "Why are you leaving?"

The stranger says, "I was just dropping something off. I have to get back to work. Don't worry; it's plenty of people and food. You'll have a good time. Chris said his sister Keisha is coming to bring you guys to the back."

Angie says, "Thank you!"

Sheryl says, "That was good timing. A spot right in front."

Keisha walks around from the back and says, "Hi! Are you Sheryl?"

Angie replies, "No. That's Sheryl. I'm Angie."

Keisha says, "How are you ladies doing? I'm Keisha, Chris's sister. Did you have a hard time finding the street?"

Sheryl assures her, "Not at all. I know the area."

Keisha asks, "Did you guys bring swimsuits to get in the pool?"

Sheryl replies, "No, not this time. Maybe next time."

Keisha says, "How do you guys know Chris? From work?"

Sheryl says, "We're just associates from out and about."

Keisha says, "Well, come on. He's on the phone right now. Watch your step. He needs to get this fixed. Here he is; just wait here. He'll be with you in one moment."

Angie and Sheryl say, "Okay. Thanks, Keisha."

Keisha replies, "No problem."

Chris calls, "I'll be with you guys in one second. Hold on."

Sheryl says, "You're good, Chris. Take your time."

Chris says, "I'm actually done now. Hey, what's up, Sheryl?"

Sheryl replies, "Hey, Chris. This is my girl Angie, Angie, this is Chris."

Angie says, "Hi, Chris. I've heard some nice things about you. Thank you for lending an ear to my girl last night at the Dragon."

Chris says, "It was nothing. How are you feeling today, Sheryl?"

Sheryl replies, "I'm doing much better."

Chris says, "I see you ladies met my sister Keisha."

Angie says, "Yes; she brought us to the back."

Chris says to Keisha, "Thanks for bringing them back, sis. I'll see you shortly."

Keisha says, "Okay. I have some guests waiting for me at the pool house. If you ladies would like a drink, that's where I'll be. What are you drinking?"

Sheryl asks, "Do you have Nuvo and Hennessy?"

Keisha replies, "Of course. We have everything."

Sheryl says, "Well, I'll have a Nuvo and Hennessy on the rocks, but light on the ice."

Keisha says, "What about you, Angie?"

Angie answers, "I like Remy."

Keisha says, "Would you like it on ice or straight?"

Angie says, "On ice. Thanks, Keisha."

Keisha says, "Okay. The drinks will be at the pool house. When you're ready, come get them."

Sheryl says, "Okay, we'll be down in a few. Thanks!" Then she says to Chris, "This is a nice house."

Angie says, "Everybody is so friendly."

Sheryl asks, "What type of work do you do?"

Chris replies, "I'm self-employed. I have been for six years."

Sheryl says, "Six years doing what?"

Chris tells her, "I buy buildings."

Sheryl says, "You buy buildings?"

Chris says, "Yes, I buy buildings. I knock them down and sell the scrap to various construction companies."

Angie comments, "Hey, that's what Richard Gere's character does for a living in the movie *Pretty Woman*."

Chris replies, "Actually, it is."

Sheryl says with a chuckle, "I need to watch *Pretty Woman* again because Richard Gere was paid in that movie. You living like that, Chris?"

Chris says, "Nah. I'm just living. Would you guys like a tour of the house?"

Sheryl and Angie reply, "Sure!"

Chris says, "Hold on, ladies, my phone is ringing. I have to take this call. Hello!" There's a pause. "I'll be out there in one second. Ladies, I need to handle something real quick. Feel free to give yourselves a tour. There's a bathroom right here, two more upstairs, and another in the pool house. I'll be right back."

Sheryl states, "This house is huge."

Angie replies, "It's very huge. Where do you want to go first?"

Sheryl says, "I'm not even going to tempt myself. He's married. I wonder if his wife is out here? Let's just sit by the pool and check out some sights. There's Keisha at the pool-house bar. Let's go chat with her."

Angie says, "That's cool. Look at my girl controlling her urge to take."

Sheryl says, "Whatever, Angie. Let's just go get those drinks."

Angie says, "Cool."

Sheryl calls, "Hey, Keisha, your brother has a beautiful home."

Keisha replies, "Yes, he does, and he is still working hard for it. It took him two long, aggravating years before he started seeing a profit from his investments. Here are you ladies' drinks. Remy on the rocks for you, Angie, and Hennessy and Nuvo with light ice for you, Sheryl."

Sheryl and Angie say, "Thank you, Keisha."

Sheryl says, "Your Jell-O shots look good."

Keisha says, "They are."

Sheryl asks, "Can I try one?"

Keisha says, "Sure."

Sheryl puts one back and says, "Wow, this is smooth. But I know too many of these will sneak up on you."

Keisha says, "Yes! Don't let the smoothness fool you, and don't take more than three. You'll be drunk faster than you know it. Angie, that Remy is a bad drink."

Angie replies, "Remy is what it is. I'll be sipping on this one all evening."

Keisha asks, "What type of work do you guys do?"

Sheryl replies, "Well, I work as a certified public accountant. I'm trying to branch off and become independent."

Keisha says, "Do you do taxes?"

Sheryl answers, "I sure do. I need all the extra money I can get."

Keisha says, "Okay, cool. Make sure I get a card or your number before you leave."

Sheryl says, "Here's my card. Call me when you're ready."

Keisha says, "I'll do that."

Sheryl says, "Thanks for the business, Keisha."

Angie says, "Yes. We all need our taxes done."

Sheryl says, "I know that's right."

Keisha asks, "What about you, Angie? What type of work do you do?"

Angie replies, "I'm a detective for the Boston Police Department."

Keisha exclaims, "Are you really? I've been on the job for six years now. I'm with the K-9 unit out of Area B."

Angie says, "You are?"

Keisha says, "Yes, girl. So that means that you're under Sergeant Tally."

Angie replies, "Yes! I can't stand Sergeant Tally."

Keisha warns, "Don't say that too loud, because Sergeant Tally is here."

Angie replies, "Is he really?"

Keisha says, "Yes. He attends all my brother's gatherings."

Sheryl comments, "It's a small world."

Keisha replies, "Yes, it is. Here's my card. We definitely have to hook up. I just tested for sergeant."

Angie says, "That's all politics. It's who you know, not how you score. Let me see if I can talk to someone for you."

Keisha says, "Thanks! I would greatly appreciate that."

Sheryl interrupts, "Excuse for a second, but is that Roland's friend Earl?"

Angie says, "Where?"

Sheryl says, "In the pool, with the woman in the blue swimsuit?"

Angie says, "It sure is."

Keisha asks, "Where do you guys know Earl from?"

Sheryl says, "Angie's boyfriend tried to hook us up last night, and this man turns out to be married."

Keisha says, "Yes, he is. That's his wife, the woman in the blue two-piece. They've been back and forth for about a year now. One minute they are together, the next minute they're not. I don't like his wife at all. She's always trying to break up Chris and Roland."

Angie says, "Roland! Keisha, are you saying Chris is gay?"

Sheryl adds, "Does his wife know?"

Angie retorts, "Sheryl, you did not hear what Keisha said, girl. Chris has a husband!"

Keisha says, "Yes. His name is Roland."

Angie asks, "Keisha, do you know Roland?"

Keisha replies, "I know Roland. Chris and Roland have been married for about one year now. I'm sorry; I thought you guys knew Chris was gay."

Sheryl says, "Wow! Chris's fine ass is gay? When? How? Why? I don't believe this!"

Keisha says, "Here he comes now."

Chris says, "What's up, people? Why the faces?"

Keisha replies, "Apparently they did not know you're gay. I'm also guessing that Angie believes her Roland is your Roland."

Chris says with a disturbed look, "Excuse me? Why would you think that my Roland is your man, Angie?"

Angie asks, "Where is he now, Chris?"

Chris says, "That was him who paged me to the front. He had an attitude when he pulled up. He was screaming about a silver Escalade in his parking spot."

Angie says, "That's Sheryl's truck. Roland knows her truck, and he knows if she's here, I'm here."

Sheryl says, "I told you, Angie. Today you find out that your Roland is a mutt. I knew something was wrong with that dude. He was just too damn perfect."

Angie replies, "Don't start with me, Sheryl. Where did he go, Chris?"

Chris says, "I don't know. He just took off."

Sheryl repeats, "He just took off?"

Angie asks, "Did he go to the Park Plaza last night for a fund-raiser?"

Chris confirms, "He sure did."

Angie says, "What did he wear?"

Chris says, "I'm not sure because he left from his sister's house."

Keisha jumps in the conversation with, "I just got a text back from him. He said he'll be back later; he's going to get his head cut."

Angie says, "Okay, let's do this. Chris, come by my house tonight as a friend of Sheryl's."

Chris says, "Okay. We need to get to the bottom of this."

Angie says, "Here's my address. Can you read my handwriting?"

Chris replies, "Yeah, that's cool. I'll be there about ten o'clock."

Angie says, "That's a good time."

Sheryl adds, "I agree with you, Chris. We all need to get to the bottom of this."

Angie says, "Come on, Sheryl. Let's go."

Sheryl says, "Now I have reason to question Roland."

Angie says, "Sheryl, don't have me strangle you in your own truck." She smiles, but her heart's not in it.

Sheryl replies, "I'm not saying anything for now. Let's just go find him."

Angie says, "I don't believe this crap. Chris, we'll see you at ten."

Chris says, "Yes, I will be there."

Angie says, "Keisha, it was nice meeting you, girl. I'll call you."

Keisha replies, "Yes, definitely give me a call later."

Angie says, "I will."

As Angie and Sheryl walk to the truck, Sheryl says, "I want to find him now."

Angie tells her, "I'm calling and he's not picking up the phone."

Sheryl says, "Angie, don't even trip. We got this. We're going to fix his butt. You have my keys?"

Angie says, "Yes. I put them in the outside part of your bag. Let's swing by his boy's house."

Sheryl asks, "Which boy?" She starts the truck.

Angie replies, "Wayne."

Sheryl says, "You mean Wayne with the black Blazer?"

Angie says, "Yes! He stays over by Ashmont Train Staition. I don't believe this mess. Sheryl, do you really think Roland is on the down low?"

Sheryl says, "To be honest, I may have thought he was a mutt, but not a mutt on the down low."

Angie says, "I don't see any of their cars out here. Let's roll through 'the Bricks.'"

They drive to that Mattapan neighborhood, and Sheryl says, "I don't see his car around here either."

Angie says, "Let's go by the Brown's Barber Shop. He's probably over there getting his hair cut."

So they drive to Brown's, and Sheryl says, "His car is not out here either."

Angie commands, "Park. I'm going inside to ask if they've seen him."

Sheryl says, "Cool. Let's go."

Angie knocks on the back door, and Steve the barber says, "Come on in, Angie and Sheryl. Long time no see. What's going on?"

Angie greets both barbers on duty. "Hey, what's up, Brian? Hey, Steve. Have you guys seen Roland?"

Steve replies, "Not since yesterday. He came through to get his hair cut, and I haven't seen him since. Why? What's up? Are you good, Angie?"

Angie says, "I'm good. I'm just looking for him. If you see him, tell him that I'm looking for him."

Brian the barber says, "Of course. I'll let him know."

Angie says, "Thanks. I'll see you guys later."

Brian says, "I got you. Hey, make sure you guys come through the block picnic for the Fourth of July. Everybody comes through. I promise you'll have a good time."

Sheryl replies, "I'll make sure we come through this year."

Angie says, "Good night." Outside the barber shop, she thinks for a minute, then says, "Sheryl, let's pass by Simco's on the bridge, but go down Norfolk Street to hit Blue Hill."

As they drive down Morton Street coming up to the light at Morton St. and Norfolk, Sheryl says, "Look, Angie! That's his car there, right?"

Angie asks, "Where?"

Sheryl says, "In the Walgreens parking lot."

Angie says, "That is his car! Pull in the parking lot. I'm going inside to talk to him. Give me the keys to the truck."

Sheryl replies, "Huh?"

Angie says, "Here are my keys to his car. Take his car and go to your house. I'll meet you there in your truck in fifteen minutes."

Sheryl says, "Okay, I got you. I'll see you shortly."

Angie says, "Hey, wait until I get to the door first to make sure he's not coming out before you take off."

Sheryl replies, "All right."

As Angie walks into the store, she thinks, "Where is he? I know he's in here. I don't care who he's with. I know he's in here. Aha, there he goes." Out loud, she says, "Hi, baby."

Roland says, "Hey. What's up, babe?"

Angie answers, "Nothing much. I've been looking for you. Where you been?"

Roland says, "I was by Mom's house earlier, helping her move some furniture around."

Angie says, "Baby, I've been calling and paging you since about four o'clock. I even dropped by Brian's spot to see if you were getting your hair cut."

Roland replies, "Sorry, baby. I left my phone at the house. What's up?"

Angie tells him, "Sheryl and a friend are coming over around ten. Can you come by? Maybe we can play some spades or dominoes."

Roland says, "Sure, babe. That's cool. I'll come through."

Angie says, "Cool beans, babe. I'll see you about ten p.m."

Roland says, "That's cool. You may see me earlier."

Angie replies, "Okay. What are you about to do now?"

Roland says, "I just need to catch up with Larry to see what's up with this personal training. You know I'm trying to get my sexy on this summer."

Angie says, "Tell Larry I said hello."

Roland says, "Will do. Hey, do I need to pick up anything?"

Angie replies, "No. I'm picking up the last of the little things I need now." Angie's phone rings and she says, "Hold on, Roland, let me answer this call. Hello?"

Sheryl asks, "Did you find him?"

Angie replies, "Yeah. I'm leaving now."

Sheryl says, "Call me right back."

Angie hangs up and tells Roland, "Sorry about that. Sheryl was asking me about tonight."

Roland says, "All right. I'll see you then."

Angie gives Roland the church hug and avoids his lips. Roland asks, "What's up with the church hug? And you turned your head. I can't get a kiss?"

Angie says, "It's not that, baby. I just have a lot on my mind. I'll talk to you about it later."

Roland replies, "I'll see you later, babe."

Angie says, "Smooches."

As Angie walks out the door, she calls Sheryl and says, "Where you at?"

Sheryl replies, "I'm just pulling up at the house."

Angie says, "Cancel meeting me at the house and just meet me in front of the Strand Theater."

Sheryl says, "What? I'm not about to get arrested driving around in this man's car, Angie. He'll be calling the police any minute."

Angie tells her, "Just stay at your spot. I'll drive Roland's car, and you follow me. He wants to play games, I got a game for him."

Angie pulls up in Sheryl's truck and gets out. She swaps keys with Sheryl. "Come on, girl. Follow me."

Sheryl asks, "What are you doing?"

Angie says, "I'm donating his car."

Sheryl exclaims, "What? You're donating his car?"

Angie replies, "Yes. I'm going to drop it off by the park."

Sheryl warns, "Girl, you know they will steal it from there."

Angie smiles. "Exactly. But they don't need to steal it. I'm giving it to whomever."

Sheryl says, "You're scaring me. You are really crazy. Are you okay, girl?"

Angie replies, "I'm fine. I just don't believe this mess. Here we go." With Sheryl following, Angie drives Roland's car to the park and hops out. When Sheryl joins her, Angie says, "Watch and learn. This is a hot spot for auto theft. I'm just going to leave the radio on and the engine running. Somebody will claim it."

Sheryl asks, "Are you sure you want to do this?"

Angie says, "It's done. Come on, girl, let's go."

Sheryl tells her, "You're straight ghetto! Don't mess around and lose your job behind this mess. How did you make damn detective?"

Angie replies, "I passed the test like the next man did. Roland have me so upset now. He must have me twisted."

Sheryl says, "I told you, men are all the same. Angie, did I ever pay you back that money I owed you?"

Angie says, "What money?"

Sheryl admits, "I don't know. I'm just checking. I don't want my stuff coming up missing."

Sheryl and Angie pull up at Angie's place. Sheryl says, "Larry and Roland are here already. He must have called Larry to come get him from Walgreens. I bet he is mad about his car."

Angie says, "He'll be okay. After tonight, he'll have other things to worry about."

Sheryl agrees, "I know that's right."

The girls go into Angie's place. Larry says, "What's up?"

Sheryl replies, "Hi, Larry, how have you been?"

Larry says, "I'm good, just taking it easy. How you been, Sheryl?"

Sheryl says, "Just working. Let me know if you need your taxes done."

Larry says, "Yeah, you have my business. I'll let you know when I'm ready. How are you, Angie?"

Angie tells him, "I'm good."

Larry asks, "How's the crime game treating you?"

Angie says, "I'm doing fine. No complaints."

Larry says, "When you guys need some training, hit me up. Roland, call me later and we'll finish up then."

Roland replies, "Cool. I'll call you tomorrow, thanks man, good look."

Larry says, "No problem. We'll get up. You guys have a good night."

Sheryl and Angie say, "Bye, Larry!"

Roland turns to Angie and says, "Baby, somebody stole my car at Walgreens!"

Angie says, "Are you serious?"

Roland says, "I'm mad."

Angie asks, "Did you call it in?"

Roland says, "Yes. I filed the police report already. Larry took me down there to do that. I just put that stereo system in. I just bought those rims and got that paint job. I tell you, it's always something."

Angie says, "Relax, baby. We'll get it back."

Roland says, "It's not just that. I only had coverage three insurance on it. I'm going to take a big loss. Listen, I just want to eat now and spend time with you, baby. I'm ready to eat. Sheryl, so who's your friend?"

Sheryl says, "His name is Chris. I just met him, so I really don't know him yet, but I do like him."

Roland says, "Good for you."

Sheryl tells him, "I'm sorry about your car."

Roland replies, "It's cool. I know I should have waited before putting all that work into that car."

Angie comments, "Baby, that's why it's best to keep a low profile. You know, like *on the down low*. Don't worry. I'll do a search tomorrow." Sheryl snickers.

Roland says, "Man, it's always something. This is not funny, Sheryl."

Sheryl answers, "I know. I'm not laughing at your situation. I was just thinking about Angie falling down. When we dropped her car off, she fell on her butt getting out of it."

Angie says, "I see we still have jokes."

Roland asks, "Baby, did you hurt yourself?"

Angie says, "Nah, I'm good."

Roland says, "So, Sheryl, where did you meet your friend?"

Sheryl replies, "I met him at the Dragon the other night."

Roland says, "You're meeting guys at fast food spots now?"

Sheryl says, "I met him after I left the Plaza from meeting your sorry boy Earl."

Roland says, "I'm sorry about that. I thought Earl and his wife were separated. That's why I thought nothing of it. I don't know who's more insane about it, you or Angie."

Sheryl replies with a smile, "Oh, it's Angie—trust me!"

Roland says, "You blitzed on Earl. I was, like, wow. I've never seen that side of you."

Sheryl says, "There's plenty sides of *us* you have not seen."

Roland replies, "Of *us*? What do you mean, *us*?"

Angie replies, "Nothing, baby. Sheryl is just being silly. You know how she is, always barking about nothing."

Roland says, "Baby, I'm hungry. I haven't had anything to eat all day. What can I snack on until the food is ready?"

Angie says, "Baby, relax. The food will be ready in about twenty minutes. Here's the remote until then."

Roland says, "Come on, ladies, I'm starving now. Hey, someone's knocking at the door."

Sheryl replies, "That should be my friend. Answer it."

Roland walks to the door. Sheryl and Angie watch him to catch the surprised look on Roland's face as he opens the door for his alleged lover. Roland says, "Hey, what's up? You must be Sheryl's friend Chris. What's good? I'm Roland."

Chris says, "What's up, Roland? Yes, I'm Chris." Seeing Sheryl, he immediately adds, "Sheryl, I have an emergency I have to get to. I was right down the street when I got the news, so I decided to drop by instead of calling you. Can you guys excuse me and Sheryl for a quick second?"

Roland replies, "Of course."

Chris walks Sheryl outside and says, "That's not my Roland."

Back in the house, Angie says, "What's up with Chris?"

Roland asks, "What do you mean? I don't know. He just called Sheryl outside, saying something about an emergency."

Angie replies, "Roland, you're looking me dead in my face and telling me you don't know Chris?"

Roland replies, "Babe, I don't know everybody. What's gotten into you? What's up?"

Angie says, "Nothing, baby."

Chris and Sheryl walk back into the house. Chris says, "Hey, Angie, I'm sorry, but I have to run. Roland, it was nice meeting you."

Roland says, "Okay. I hope all is well with the family. Quick question—are you the same Chris who was featured in last month's 'Who's Who' column in the paper?"

Chris replies, "Yeah, they did a brief article on me."

Roland says, "That was a nice piece. You buy buildings and sell the scrap, right?"

Chris says, "Exactly! Again, it's nice to meet you, but I have to run."

Roland says, "Cool. We'll get up. Man, go handle your business."

Chris announces, "I'm out. Later, people." He closes the door behind him.

Angie says, "Guys, I think I'm going to be sick. Sheryl, can I talk to you for a second in the bathroom?"

Roland says in exasperation, "Can I get some food, please? Hello?" The girls ignore him.

In the bathroom, Sheryl says, "Girl, they don't know each other."

Angie says, "Yeah, I sort of figured that out. Damn!"

Sheryl's cell rings. She answers and Chris says, "What's up? Does your girl feel better now?"

Sheryl replies, "Angie was so pissed off that she gave Roland's car away earlier tonight!"

Chris says, "She did what?"

Sheryl repeats, "She gave his car away."

Chris asks, "What do you mean, 'gave his car away'?"

Sheryl tells him, "We just took it somewhere and left it running."

Chris says, "When did you do this, and why?"

Sheryl says, "It was about an hour ago, after we left your house. She was angry about him being involved with you."

Chris says, "Y'all are straight crazy. Oh, my. Y'all are shell for that."

Sheryl replies, "Chris, you have to help me try to get it back."

Chris says, "Yes, we need to do that right now. If it were my car, I'd be kicking y'all's you-know-whats right now. I'm turning around. Come downstairs in about ten minutes."

Sheryl says, "I'll tell Angie."

Chris says, "Y'all are crazy. I can hang with y'all chicks. I'll be outside shortly."

Roland knocks on the bathroom door and asks Angie to open it. Sheryl replies, "She'll be out in a second." Then Sheryl says to Angie, "Chris and I are going to look for the car."

Angie tells her, "Don't bother. It's probably stripped by now, or it's out for a joyride."

Sheryl insists, "Girl, we're going to look for it anyway."

Angie says, "I feel so bad. What am I going to do?"

Roland shouts, "I'm about to raid your cabinets and cook my own food!"

Sheryl calls back, "That's cool. Make yourself at home."

Roland says, "Are you serious? I'm about to cook a full-course meal."

Angie says to Sheryl, "I need to talk to him. He won't forgive me for this."

Sheryl replies, "Don't tell him."

Angie says, "I have to, Sheryl. Our relationship is built on trust. How am I going to be able to look my man in the face, knowing what I did?"

Sheryl says, "Just don't tell him tonight. I got your back. I'll handle him for now. Don't worry, Angie. I'll tell him something. I'll talk with you later. Go lie down."

Angie says, "Thanks, Sheryl. I'll talk to you in a few."

Sheryl replies, "Give me a hug, girl. It's going to be all right. I'll call you shortly."

Sheryl comes out of the bathroom and says, "Roland, can I speak to you for a second?"

Roland says, "Hold up. I have something to tell you guys first."

Sheryl asks, "What's that?"

Roland says, "Is she going to come out of the bathroom?"

Sheryl says, "She has some woman things going on right now. She may be a while, so go ahead and eat. Just give her a few. What's up? I have to go meet Chris and make sure he's good with his situation."

Roland tells her, "Well, I just bought a house for my baby."

Sheryl says, "You just what?"

Roland replies, "Yes! I just bought a house she said she wanted. I qualified for the mortgage and I'm surprising her tonight. I'm also proposing to her tonight."

Sheryl says, "What?"

Roland says, "I've been thinking about it for some time now. Check out the ring. You like it?"

Sheryl exclaims, "Oh, my God, that's beautiful! I'm so happy for you guys."

Roland says, "I can't wait to show her the house. It's a new split-level in Milton."

Sheryl says, "You've been doing the damn thing, I see."

Roland replies, "I've been saving. I was just waiting for the right time, and that right time is tonight. But I'm nervous, Sheryl. I'm scared she might say no because of her career."

Sheryl says, "Roland, I don't think you have anything to worry about. Angie is crazy about you! Plus, that three carat diamond ring will cheer her up. And a house! That's sure to keep her panties wet." She pauses, then adds, "I am sorry about your car."

Roland says, "I'm not tripping about that. Material things go and come. I was about to sell it anyway. That's why I put the work into it. I can always buy another car. Even though I only have cover three on it, I have store insurance on all my rims and stereo. Thank God. Now, what's up, Sheryl? What do you have to tell me?"

Sheryl replies, "I don't know how to tell you this, but your girl thinks she's pregnant. Don't tell her I told you. She just needs a little time to gather herself. You know, she's at a point in her career where she's not ready for a child yet."

Roland says, "Really! We think we may be having a child? That's the best news I heard all month. The timing is just right! I'm so excited. Let me gather myself and pretend as if I don't know about it. I'm so happy Sheryl. Thanks for sharing!"

Sheryl says, "Wow, I'm glad to see you so happy and excited Roland."

Roland says, "Yes! Yes! Yes!"

Sheryl responds, "Roland, whatever she tells you tonight, you have to be supportive of her, Roland. She may even tell you that she needs to get away for a week or two. If so, let her go. Allow her to come to you when she's ready to talk to you. The two of you need each other right now. I'm off to meet Chris. I'll talk to you later—and congratulations, boy. I'm so happy for you guys."

Roland says, "All right. I'll do that. Thanks for the talk. I'll see you later."

Sheryl goes on her way. Roland demands that Angie come out of the bathroom and talk to him. He says, "Are you okay? Whatever is troubling you tonight, don't worry about it. Just know that I have your back whatever it is. I love you. But listen, I'm hungry. What do you say we go get something to eat and take it in for the night?"

Angie answers, "Yes, baby. What do you want to eat?"

Roland says, "We're heading straight to my spot."

Angie says, "Where? Simco's?"

Roland replies, "You know it."

The next morning, Angie calls Sheryl as Angie gets ready for work. "What's up, girl? What the hell did you tell Roland?"

Sheryl retorts, "What did he tell you?"

Angie says, "Nothing. He was just normal Roland, doing what I love about him."

Sheryl says, "What's that?"

Angie says, "Being supportive and looking out for my best interest. I know he was upset about his car last night. But he was more concerned about me. What did you tell him?"

Sheryl answers, "I told him that you might be pregnant."

Angie replies, "What? You told him what?"

Sheryl says, "It just came out. I said you *might* be pregnant, so it can be a false alarm. You have a loophole, so you're good. I didn't know what else to say."

Angie says, "You could have told him anything except that. How did he respond, Sheryl? What did he say?"

Sheryl says, "Before he spoke, I also told him that you were under a lot of pressure. That he should wait until you were ready to speak to him about it. Plus, you needed to get away or spend some time by yourself."

Angie asks, "What did he say to that?"

Sheryl says, "Girl, he was so excited about you being pregnant, I could have told him what you did last night and it wouldn't have mattered. That's how excited he was."

Angie replies, "Was he?"

Sheryl says, "I can say that man really cares for you, Angie, but I know there's a mutt in that man somewhere."

Angie says, "Whatever, girl. He's been good to me. Any luck on the car?"

Sheryl says, "Chris and I looked all night, and nothing. Roland said he was about to sell it, and he does have insurance on the rims and stereo."

Angie says, "He does?"

Sheryl affirms, "That's what he said."

Angie asks, "What else did he say?"

Sheryl replies, "Nothing. He was full of joy when I told him that you was pregnant."

Angie says, "Thanks, girl. Let me finish getting ready for work. It's one of those days. I should call out but I'm going to go in, I have some paper work to finish up. I'll speak with you later. Bye, sweetie."

Sheryl replies, "Bye-bye."

Angie walks into her bedroom and surprises Roland. "Roland? You still sleeping? Maybe this will wake you up."

Roland replies, "Baby, what are you doing? See, you're always starting stuff. It's eight o'clock and you're a hell of an alarm."

Angie says, "I know, right? Let's go to Brother's for breakfast. I want to talk to you. I'm going to call in and take a sick day."

Roland says, "I already know that you might go on vacation for a week or two. Plus you might be pregnant!"

Angie says, "Oh, Sheryl's got a big mouth."

Roland says, "She told me last night before she left to meet Chris."

Angie says, "She's always running her mouth."

Roland agrees, "That's your girl. But she always has your back, no matter what."

Angie says, "I know. Come on. Can we go to Brother's anyway?"

Roland says, "Yeah. Give me about ten minutes. I'm getting up."

A little while later, they arrive at Brother's Restaurant. Angie says, "I hope it's not crowded. Find a table, baby. I'll order. What do you want?"

Roland says, "Baby, order me scrambled eggs hard with cheese, beef sausage, grits, and biscuits with some strawberry jelly."

Angie says, "Okay. I think I'll order the same."

Roland replies, "Is a window seat cool?"

Angie says, "Yeah, baby, that table is fine."

Roland goes over to the table. A few minutes later, Angie joins him. Roland asks, "Baby, what did you order?"

Angie says, "I ordered what you ordered, except I got my eggs scrambled hard with cheese."

Roland says, "I guess we beat the rush crowd."

Angie says, "I guess we did. The food looks and smells good."

Roland asks, "What did you get to drink?"

Angie replies, "I didn't. What do you want?"

Roland says, "Order me an OJ, baby?"

Just then, a voice from the counter calls their order number. Angie says, "They're calling us for the food already?"

Roland says, "I'll get the food. Go ahead and get the drinks."

As she arrives back at the table, Angie says, "Yes, the food looks good. Give me your hand, baby, so I can bless the food. Dear heavenly Father, we thank you for allowing us to be blessed with another day. We thank you for blessing our family and friends as well. Thank you for allowing us to nourish our bodies this morning. We ask you to watch over us today as we practice our chosen desires, and give us favor. We ask you to please bless the food that we're about to eat. Again, we thank you for another day. Amen. Amen."

Roland asks, "Baby, how many months along do you think we are?"

Angie replies, "I don't know. I just had morning sickness once."

Roland says, "Well, I'll tell you this, sweetie. I'm ready for family and I'm happy."

Angie retorts, "I hope you are! Hearing that makes me feel so good Roland. I love you!"

Roland says, "I know you probably think that this is bad timing with your career and all, but I know we can do this."

Angie asks, "Do you really think that, Roland?"

Roland says, "Really, I do. That's why I think it's about time for us to take it to another level. We've been together for a while now, and I've never been happier. How do you feel about what we have?"

Angie replies, "I feel good, baby. I'm very happy with you and what we have."

Roland says, "I'm ready to move to the next stage in caring about and loving you."

Angie says, "Roland, you're scaring me. Are you doing what I think you're doing?"

Roland tells her, "Angie, we've been together for three years, and you have become my best friend. You complete me in every way. I love you, Angie Coleman. Would you marry me?" He opens the jeweler's box and presents her with the three carat diamond ring.

Angie says, "Baby, I love you so much. I'm the happiest woman in world. Yes, I'll marry you."

After he puts the ring on her finger, Roland says, "Baby, I was debating on asking you."

Angie asks, "Why?"

Roland says, "Baby, I've never felt so scared before in my life. From this point on, it's all about me and you."

Angie says, "Yes, baby, it's all about me and you. And I have something to tell you. You might change your mind after hearing this."

Roland says, "It can't be that serious."

Angie replies, "Oh, this is very serious, baby."

Roland says, "I'm listening."

Angie says, "I took your car from Walgreens and purposely left it unattended so it could be stolen."

Roland screams, "*What*? Why would you do that? You took my car and did what?"

Angie admits, "Baby, I thought you were on the down low."

Roland says, "You thought I was *what*, Angie?"

Angie says it again. "I thought you were on the down low."

Roland says, "Why in hell would you think that?"

Angie says, "I don't know. I'm sorry for doubting you, baby. That's not it, though; there's more."

Roland repeats, "There's more?"

Angie replies, "Yes! Sheryl and I thought you were living a double life, married to her friend Chris."

Roland says, "Huh? You mean the Chris from last night? I wish I had his money. Angie, this is classic. I don't understand where any of this is coming from."

Angie says, "It's a long story."

Roland replies, "I don't think I want to hear any more."

Angie asks, "Baby, do you hate me now?"

Roland kisses her on the forehead and says, "Hate you? Babe, this mess is funny. I'm laughing at you right now. The car can be replaced; that's not a big deal. I probably would have done worse, had I thought you were involved with another man."

Angie says, "Oh, really? I guess we'll never know."

Roland says, "However, I am disappointed you decided not to talk to me before you acted. Remember, baby, communication is key. You should always feel comfortable talking to me about anything. You are my best friend, and I'm still learning you. I love you, girl! Don't you ever doubt me and not get the clarity that you deserve. Do you understand me?"

Angie replies, "Yes, baby. I love you so much. But just to let you know—if you had started tripping, you were not getting the ring back!"

Roland says, "Oh, I was getting it back. Trust, as you and Sheryl say. I love these scrambled eggs. And in regards to the car, you actually did us a favor!"

Angie asks, "What do you mean?"

Roland says, "I have a partner who can take care of my insurance papers. I'll see if he can make the situation work out for the better. We can use the money to split some bills up."

Angie says, "I know that's right!"

Roland adds, "That reminds me, you have to meet someone after we finish eating."

Angie says, "Really? Who is it?"

Roland tells her, "You'll see."

Angie says excitedly, "Come on! I'm done eating. Are you ready?"

Roland says, "In a few. Remember last night? I was starving, and my Simco's did not do the job. Let me enjoy this moment, babe."

Angie says, "I'm too excited. Hurry and finish eating so we can go, baby."

Roland replies in his Mack voice, "Be cool, baby. Finish your food up."

Angie repeats, "I'm too excited. Where are we going? Can you give me a clue? Where is it?"

Roland says, "It's in Milton."

Angie says, "Milton! Baby, I'm lost. Nothing is in Milton."

Roland says, "Relax. I told you, I have a friend for you to meet. Come on. Let's get out of here."

As they drive through Mattapan Square heading into Milton, Angie says, "They need to put steady lights at this intersection, as opposed to these flashing lights."

Roland says, "I know that's right! They had four accidents at this intersection last month. Ten minutes up the road, we'll be at our destination."

Angie muses, "I'm curious about who this person is that I'm meeting."

Roland says, "After we leave here, we're going straight to the car wash. How do you let your car get so dirty?"

Angie says, "Baby, it just sits at headquarters. I drive the company car like it's my own. I have not had my car detailed in about three months now."

Roland says, "I see. That Charger over there is nice."

Angie says, "That's Detective L. Bullard with the Milton Police Department. He's cool."

Roland says, "I wonder if it's fast?"

Angie replies, "Yes, it's fast."

Roland says, "I see all types of nice unmarked cars now."

Angie says, "They buy them from auctions of seized property."

Roland says, "I heard that, but wasn't sure it was true."

Angie offers, "I can ask my captain to get something you might like. What kind of car do you want next?"

Roland replies, "I'm getting an SUV."

Angie says, "Oh, okay. Which one? There are so many SUVs to choose from."

Roland says, "I like that Lincoln Navigator L and the Lexus truck. Oh yes, I like the Lexus truck."

Angie says, "The Lexus."

Roland says, "Yes, the Lexus truck."

Angie asks, "Which color will you get?"

Roland replies, "If I can afford it, I'll get it in an onyx black or a Pepsi blue."

Angie says, "I don't think my captain can get one of those, but you and I can buy one together."

Roland says, "We'll talk about it. We have some other matters on the plate for now, but yes, in the near future."

Angie changes the subject. "Baby, I really thought you were going to hate me after what I told you I did."

Roland replies, "Oh, don't think you're off the hook. You will be making up for that one. But I don't want to talk about that right now."

Angie asks, "Can we talk about this person we're going to meet?"

Roland says, "Well, we're here now. I wonder if she's home?"

Angie says, "Who, baby?"

Roland says, "Your surprise!"

Angie says, "I don't know anyone who lives here. Who is it?"

Roland replies, "Shhh. Come on; you'll soon see. Ring the doorbell."

Angie says, "This house is nice. Who can this be? I see someone coming now. That's a white woman you're bugging. I don't know this woman."

Roland says, "Relax, sweetie."

The mysterious woman comes to the door and says, "Hi! How are you guys doing? You must be Roland's fiancée, Angie?"

Angie says, "Yes, I'm Angie. How did you know that? He just proposed not even thirty minutes ago. Who are you?"

The mysterious woman says, "I'm Ms. Brook, your real estate agent."

Angie repeats, "My real estate agent?"

Ms. Brook says, "Yes. Welcome to your new home."

Angie turns to Roland and says, "Baby, this is *our* new home?"

Roland replies, "Yes!"

Angie says, "I love it! And I love you so much. I'm sorry for thinking you were on the down low."

Ms. Brooks gives Angie a quick, confused look. Roland states, "It's a long story that I don't even want to hear about."

Angie says, "Baby, I just feel so bad about it."

Roland says, "But how do you feel now about your new home?"

Angie says, "Oh, my God. I'm so excited. I feel like a baby in a toy store."

Ms. Brooks says, "Would you like a tour, Angie?"

Angie says, "Yes! Yes! Yes! Please show me our new home."

Ms. Brooks says, "It's a split-level house plan that is a variation of a ranch style. Rather than one level, split-levels have rooms at varying heights."

Angie says, "Wow, baby, this is really nice."

Ms. Brooks continues, to say, "Garages in split-level homes are often tucked beneath living space. Basements in split-level floor plans have above-ground windows, providing lots of sunlight into the lower levels. Roland told me that you love plants."

Angie says, "Yes, I do."

Ms. Brooks says, "Well, this house with its well-lighted basement will be ideal for your plants."

Angie replies, "I'm at a loss for words, Ms. Brooks. I don't know what to say other then it is so beautiful."

Roland says, "I'm glad you like it."

Angie says, "What do I need to do to make this happen?"

Roland says, "Babe, the home is ours. We own it!"

Angie asks, "How?"

Roland says, "Our mortgage is only twelve hundred a month. You tell me—can we afford it?"

Angie replies, "Yes, baby. Yes, we can!"

Roland says, "I know. I had Ms. Brook do all the research and work out all the details. Everything is good."

Angie says, "Baby, this is my dream house."

Roland asks, "Guess what?"

Angie says, "Now what?"

Roland says, "Here are your keys. You can move in today. I already hired movers to pick up our things on the twenty-third."

Angie exclaims, "That's tomorrow! I love you and everything about you, baby. I'm sorry for ever doubting your manhood."

Roland says, "Yeah, that's another topic to be discussed at a later date. This is why my phone was off yesterday when you were calling. I was closing the deal on the house. Not because I was on the down low with your boy Chris."

Angie says, "Baby, this is too much. I'm really sorry. I'll make it up to you."

Roland replies, "No need, Angie. You saying yes was enough."

Angie repeats, "I love you, baby."

Roland says, "I love you more. Baby, can I use your car? I need to meet Larry."

Angie says, "Yes, baby. I'll call Sheryl."

Roland says, "Sounds like a plan."

Ms. Brook says, "Here come the guys who are treating the pool."

Angie asks, "The pool?"

Ms. Brooks says, "Yes, the swimming pool!"

Angie says to Roland, "Baby, we have a pool here as well?"

Roland replies, "Yes. Ms. Brooks will show you. I've got to run."

Angie says, "I love you so much. Go do you, baby. Go do you. What do you want to eat tonight?"

Roland says, "Oh, it's like that? You're asking me what I want to eat?"

Angie says, "Of course. You're my fiancée now. So what do you want to eat?"

Roland says, "Surprise me, baby."

Angie says, "Okay. I'll do just that and surprise you."

Roland says, "I'll be back about seven. Talk to you later."

Angie kisses him and says, "I love you, baby."

Roland says, "I love you more."

Watching him leave, Ms. Brooks says, "You have a good man there, Angie."

Angie replies, "Yes, he is, and he's my everything."

Ms. Brooks says, "Congratulations on your new home. Here are your keys. This is the code for the alarm. Press command, then these three numbers here. If your alarm is set off, a private security agency will respond as soon as possible. Their office is right around the corner at Adams and Dorchester. Do you have any questions?"

Angie replies, "Ms. Brooks, I'm still overwhelmed. Can I give you a call later in the week when I have time to get settled?"

Ms. Brooks says, "Absolutely. If you have any questions, here's my card. Call anytime during business hours, Monday through Friday."

Angie says, "Thank you. I will do that. You have a good day."

Ms. Brooks says, "Take care, and enjoy your new home."

As the sales agent leaves, Angie calls Sheryl to tell her the good news. "Girl, the phone rang like six times. Are you busy?"

Sheryl replies, "I'm good. What's going?"

Angie says, "You're not going to believe how my morning went."

Sheryl says, "You sound excited. What happened?"

Angie replies, "Girl, Roland proposed to me this morning in Brother's Restaurant."

Sheryl says, "For real?"

Angie says, "Yeah, girl."

Sheryl says, "Well, did you accept?"

Angie says, "Hell yeah! I even told him about the car, but we still need to talk about that one."

Sheryl tells her, "I'm happy for you, girl. I knew last night. He showed me the ring."

Angie says, "You knew?"

Sheryl says, "He told me last night, before I told him that you might be pregnant."

Angie informs her, "Well, you're about to be an auntie, because I *am* pregnant."

Sheryl shrieks, "*What?* Oh, my God. How far along are you?"

Angie replies, "I'm not positive, but I think I am about three months in. That's why I got quit when you told me you told him that. I was, like, damn, does she know? But, girl, I have something to show you."

Sheryl says, "I saw the ring, girl."

Angie says, "Not that, silly. Come by. I'm over a coworker's house and I'll show you."

Sheryl replies, "Okay, where are you at? I can only come by for a few because I have to go to work".

Angie replies, "That's cool." She gives Sheryl the directions and adds, "Girl, just put the address in your GPS."

Sheryl says, "I'll be there shortly."

Sheryl arrives at Angie's new house and rings the doorbell. "Hey, girl, what's up? Where's your car?"

Angie says, "Roland has it."

Sheryl asks, "Whose house is this?"

Angie says, "Come on in—this is our new home!"

Sheryl replies, "He actually told me about the house the other night but I did not know it was going to be this beautiful! Get out of here. Oh, my God, this is nice. I'm so happy for you! Girl, Roland is doing it like that? How's he doing this on an AutoZone salary?

Angie says, "Girl, I'm so happy!"

Sheryl says, "When did all this happen? What did he say about the car?"

Angie replies, "He did not trip. Of course he was mad. He said we'll talk about it later."

Sheryl says, "I'm impressed. Let me find out Roland thinks like an executive. Look at this house."

Angie says, "I know. It's beautiful, right?"

Sheryl asks, "Where's he at now?"

Angie says, "He's taking care of some business. Check out the swimming pool!"

Sheryl says, "Wow! I'm done. You steal this man's car, you tell him you stole it, and the same day you're in a beautiful home."

Angie smiles. "That's why he's my Roland."

Sheryl says, "I'm done with you, Angie. I have to get back to work. I'll see you later when I get off work."

Angie says, "Okay, cool. Can you help me move some things later?"

Sheryl says, "Yeah. I'll talk to you when I get off. I'm so happy for you, girl."

Angie replies, "Okay, hit me up and I'll talk to you later."

Sheryl says, "Bye, girl."

Sheryl arrives at work and looks for her diary. She thinks, "Where is it? I know it's in my desk somewhere. Ah, here it is. Still brand new. I guess it's time to start writing."

Diary Entry 1:

My girl Angie finally found her happiness. I always knew Roland was a good man, but I never knew he had that in him. What's my problem? Where's my happiness? Where's my man? I wonder if the church is still having singles conventions.

It's time for me to try to find myself and pray for my happiness. Maybe that's where I'm going wrong. I'm looking for it as opposed to allowing it to happen naturally. I'm so happy for her, but I don't understand.

My girl Angie stole her man's car and just left it running in a strange neighborhood. That's deep. A good man is hard to find. If I had done something like that with my luck, I can only imagine. I need to experience what it's like to have a man—a good man. I have everything I can ask for except my happiness. That was the truth when they said "Money can't buy happiness, just material things, more bills, and a life filled with dishonest friends."

I'm sure someone is out there for me. I just need to get myself together. Make it happen. Maybe, if I joined a gym or some type of martial arts school, as opposed to just going to a church, I can meet someone. In the last year and a half, I've had five relationships and have gone on numerous dates. I give up. I don't see myself dating anyone in my near future.

Do I need a man in my life? It seems as if I don't, but I know there's someone for everybody. Men are the backbones to our families, best friends, security, and much more. With some grooming, support, guidance, and communication, we might just become a little bit happier in our relationships.

I experienced my father treating my mother like a prostitute. I've seen my father make my mom sell her body on various street corners in LA on many occasions. I never got a chance to know my mother.

My father always had different women in and out of the house. Fortunately for myself, I had a neighbor who allowed me to stay with her through my high school years until I went off to college here on the East Coast. I was scared of my father. He called me his little California Sunshine, but I never knew what he meant.

Bitter Gets Better

> *I thought as I got older that my father was going to have me working on the streets. I'm thankful for my neighbor allowing me to stay over at her house while my parents were out and about. I'm sure my neighbor was blessed in her endeavors for opening her door to me.*

Someone knocks on Sheryl's office door, and she discontinues writing in her diary.

Chapter 5

The Proposal

Later that evening, Sheryl arrives at Angie's new place and rings the doorbell. Angie says, "Hey, girl. Did you have a hard time finding it?"

Sheryl replies, "No; it was easy to find. I'm so happy for you. Roland had to be planning for this for a while."

Angie says, "Of course. He's downstairs hooking up wires for the flat screen, so he can watch his football and basketball games."

Sheryl says, "Wait a minute—is this a pool in the backyard? I thought you meant a little fish pond or something. You have an actual swimming pool! What is Roland doing on the side?"

Roland comes upstairs and says, "Hey, what's up, Sheryl? How do you like the house?"

Sheryl replies, "It's nice. What are you doing on the side? I know AutoZone is not paying for this."

Roland says, "Something on the side? Girl, you're tripping. It's called good credit and proper planning with a good real estate agent. I just worked and saved. Anything is possible with a budget."

Angie agrees, "That is true."

Sheryl says, "Well, I'm so happy for you guys. You plan on moving some things tonight?"

Roland says, "No; the movers are coming tomorrow."

Angie says, "Tonight we were going to discuss the car situation."

Roland says, "Both of you thought I was on the down low?"

Sheryl replies, "Roland, I just couldn't imagine you getting down like that. It was the way things came into play."

Angie says, "That's what you were laughing about the other night."

Sheryl says, "I was thinking about you and Chris being together."

Roland says, "Oh, you guys think that's funny?"

Sheryl replies, "It was just coincidence. You were both named Roland. You both went to the fund-raiser. The other Roland got mad when my truck was parked in his parking spot, like he knew whose truck it was. The list goes on and on. Even Chris was worried. We all thought we were putting it together, but it backfired on all of us. You might have to send Angie to those crazy folks in the psych ward!"

Angie exclaims, "Whatever, Sheryl!"

Sheryl says, "She drove your car to the park, got out of it, and just left it running. Roland, I strongly encourage you not to ever get her upset. She may turn hot pink as opposed to Hulk green, but she's just as dangerous!"

Angie laughs and says, "We have jokes, Sheryl. Don't worry. I got your back. You know what goes around comes back around."

Sheryl says, "I'm just saying you scared me straight."

Roland says, "I just don't believe you guys thought I was on the down low. It's cool, though. For the record, I'm all man. Baby, you need these ice packs now or later?"

Sheryl says, "Roland, now that was wrong."

Roland says, "My baby knows how I put it down."

Sheryl says, "That's why her butt went crazy and she did what she did. You had her butt twitching the next morning."

Angie says, "I'm going to give you guys this moment."

Sheryl asks, "So when is the date?"

Roland replies, "I'm thinking about April of next year."

Sheryl says, "Do you guys plan on having a big wedding or a small wedding?"

Angie says, "I want a big wedding."

Sheryl asks, "Have you guys picked a place yet?"

Roland tells her, "Actually, we're going to go over everything next Sunday."

Angie says, "The only thing we need to work on now is the invitation list. I think we can knock that out in a couple of days. What do you think?"

Roland says, "I think it's a done deal. Let's start the list tonight."

Angie asks Sheryl, "Can you be my maid of honor?"

Sheryl says, "Of course! Who else can it be? Let me know what you need me to do."

Angie says, "Okay. Thank you, girl. We'll talk later."

Sheryl says, "I'm about to head to my house. I might go out later. I'll call you."

Angie says, "Have a good night, girl."

Sheryl says, "Good night, guys."

Roland replies, "Good night, Sheryl, and stop meeting gay men at fast food spots."

Sheryl tells him, "Good one. I see we still got jokes. Bye, guys."

After Sheryl closes the door, Roland says, "She took off quick. What's wrong with her?"

Angie replies, "I'm not sure. I guess she really wanted to go hang out tonight."

Roland says, "Baby, that's not it. Something else is bothering Sheryl. Do you think she may be jealous of you?"

Angie says, "Of course not. I'll talk to her and find out tomorrow when I see her."

Roland says, "Baby, I'm ready to eat."

Angie says, "What?"

Roland asks, "Is the food ready yet?"

Angie replies, "No, but I am."

Roland says, "Don't play with me, Angie. I'm so hungry I can eat my food and you at the same time."

Angie exclaims, "So freaky!"

Roland says, "It is what it is. I love you, baby!"

Angie replies, "I love you too, Roland."

Meanwhile, at Sheryl's place, Sheryl looks through her black book and thinks, "Who can I call tonight? Sean is cool, but too much baby-mama drama with him. That's the last thing I need. Mike is too thuggish and hard for himself. Anthony is too pretty. Any man who takes longer than me to get dressed gets no play from me. Curtis is okay, but all he wants to do is have sex, start an argument, then leave. I have no luck with the men I meet. Well, I guess I'll curl up with another book or movie tonight. Yeah. I'll read for about an hour, and then I guess it's another diary or *Nine-Inch Wonder* night."

Diary Entry 2:

My girl is getting married to a cashier from AutoZone. She's only known him for about three years. I guess he's the man. She gave his car away and told him to his face his ass is on the down low, and she continues to be happy. He buys her a home and still loves her. Where am I going wrong? Work is good. I look good. I have a good, stable job and I have my health. I should be happy.

Maybe, I should stop thinking with my mind and allow my heart to fall in love. Yeah, right. Every fool who thinks he's looking good will be trying to run over me. Maybe I need that. I don't know. I need help. I just want to be happy. I just want to be happy. I'm going out tonight. The hell with trying to do right. It is what it is. Later for now.

Sheryl grabs her purse and decides to catch a movie in the theater. She needs to gas up, so she pulls in to a gas station. She sees an attractive man at the pump next to her. He says, "Excuse me, how are you doing?"

Sheryl says, "I'm good."

The attractive man says, "I'm Terron Can I get that for you?"

Sheryl replies, "Sure. I'm Sheryl. Thanks. Terron, do you always meet women at the gas station?"

Terron says, "I'm just saying hello and offering to pump your gas for you. Is something wrong with pumping your gas? Here, you can do it yourself."

Sheryl says, "I see you're a little rugged."

Terron says, "A woman is a lady until she treats herself different. Nah, I saw a woman I liked and decided to reach out to you. We could have been anywhere. I just like what I see! Are you married?"

Sheryl says, "I'm not. And you?"

Terron says, "I've been divorced for three years now."

Sheryl asks, "How many children do you have?"

Terron says, "I have no children. What about you, do you have children?"

Sheryl says, "I would need a husband to have children."

Terron tells her, "You're very attractive. Are you involved?"

Sheryl replies, "I'm single. How about you?"

Terron says, "I'm single myself."

Sheryl asks, "Are you single by choice or craziness?"

Terron says with a soft chuckle, "It took a while to get over my divorce, and now I'm good. Ready to get back out there and have fun again. I just hate dating."

Sheryl agrees, "So do I. What do you hate about it?"

Terron replies, "The whole process. I just be myself now. It took me some time to learn how to be myself, but I finally got it. What do you hate about dating?"

Sheryl says, "I hate the lies men tell just to try to get some."

Terron says, "To try to get some!"

Sheryl says, "Yes. You know it's true. Y'all see a big butt and all you think about is hitting it."

Again, Terron repeats, "Hitting it!"

Sheryl says, "Yes, hitting it."

Terron says, "Well, I'm a breast man myself, but a nice ass does not hurt. Let me see. Turn around."

Sheryl smacks Terron on his arm and says, "See what I mean? You're just like the rest of them—no good!"

Terron says, "I'm just playing. So what side of town do you live on?"

Sheryl says, "I stay minutes from Back Bay."

Terron says, "Whoa! How is it living downtown?"

Sheryl says, "It's active but I like it. A cluster of people who think their mess don't stink."

Terron says, "I can imagine. Are you from Boston?"

Sheryl replies, "I'm from Los Angeles, California. Where are you from?"

Terron says, "I'm from Boston. I stay here in Dorchester over by Ashmont Station. I was born and raised here. How long have you been here from California?"

Sheryl says, "I've been here for a while now. I was in Rhode Island for six years going to school, and then came to Boston afterward. I've been in the Northeast for fourteen years."

Terron asks, "What part of LA are you from?"

Sheryl replies, "I'm from South Central."

Terron says, "South Central! I heard it's tough out there."

Sheryl says, "Every state has its bad places."

Terron says, "I feel you on that one. The smell of this gas is starting to get me sick. Is it possible to give you a call later this evening?"

Sheryl demands, "Are you gay or married?"

Terron replies, "I promise you it's nothing gay about me, and as I told you, I'm divorced. It sounds like you've been through some bad relationships."

Sheryl says, "I'm good."

Terron says, "I've been through some bad experiences myself."

Sheryl says, "Like what?"

Terron says, "Well, a very bad divorce for one. I've been through enough to want to stay single."

Sheryl asks, "Are you the argumentative type?"

Terron replies, "No. I wouldn't say that I am. I just know what I want and know how I'm going to get it. For the record, I wouldn't let your number sit around for a week or two. I'm an old-school romantic—one woman at a time. Whenever I think of you, I'll make it a point to let you know that."

Sheryl says, "Oh, really?"

Terron says, "Really! I think women have to take into consideration that all men are not the same. We all, both men and women, are capable of selfishness, but we all don't practice selfish behaviors when it comes to courting. Don't look surprised. I said courting. Boys date. Some of us are still sincere, honest, thoughtful, and caring men. I'm single because of women I've experienced living in their pasts and being straight-out judgmental."

Sheryl says, "Terron, can you hold your thought? We need to pull the cars over into the parking spots. The cashier in the gas station looks as though he's on his way outside to ask us to move."

Terron replies, "Let's move to the spots on the right, and I'll hop in your truck."

Sheryl says, "That's cool."

They move their vehicles, and Terron gets in the passenger side of the Escalade. He observes, "Wow, your truck is high and big."

Sheryl says, "I like big things, I mean trucks."

Terron asks, "Are you flirting, Sheryl?"

Sheryl replies, "I am not."

Terron says, "Okay, I'll let that one go. But like I was saying, a lot of women front about their feelings. Some act like they have no interest in the men they are seeing. That's young. That's high school. I'm the type of man who is going to show my interest in someone that I'm feeling."

Sheryl says, "I like that. A little strong, but I like it. Are you always this forward?"

Terron says, "I don't think I'm forward. I just go after what I want when I want it. Listen, do you have any plans tonight? I would like to ask you out."

Sheryl says, "Ask me out! You mean now?"

Terron replies, "Yes, now."

Sheryl says, "I'm listening."

Terron says, "Would you like to go eat and then maybe see a good action movie?"

Sheryl says, "Wow, this will be a first. I guess. Why not?"

Terron says, "I'm going to the Red Box to rent the movie *Cop Out* with Bruce Willis."

Sheryl replies, "I saw that. It was a good movie."

Terron agrees, "It was. I saw it and plan on chilling tonight watching it. I'm into action movies."

Sheryl says, "So you want me to come to your house and watch a movie with you?"

Terron says, "Well, that's what I was planning prior to meeting you here at the gas station."

Sheryl replies, "I'll go out with you tonight if we go to the theater. I'm not going to your house. I'm good."

Terron says, "I feel you. Cool. Let's take one car. I stay around the corner from here. Follow me so I can park my car at home and ride with you. Have you eaten yet?"

Sheryl says, "Yeah, I'm not really hungry. I'll get some junk from the theater. Where did you want to go get something to eat?"

Terron says, "It's cool. I'm good."

As Sheryl and Terron head out in Sheryl's truck, Sheryl says, "Terron, what type of work do you do?"

Terron replies, "I'm a ninth-grade English teacher over at Madison Park High."

Sheryl asks, "Do you like it? How long have you been teaching?"

Terron says, "For six years now. It's cool. What about yourself?"

Sheryl says, "I'm a CPA."

Terron asks, "You like working with numbers?"

Sheryl says, "I have no complaints. I enjoy solving money mistakes and rendering accounts."

Terron says, "How long have you been doing that?"

Sheryl says, "About three years now."

Terron comments, "This is a nice truck you have. What are you sitting on, twenty-two-inch rims?"

Sheryl says, "Close. They're twenty-four inches, with the Nito tires."

Terron says, "Okay, big time. I see it costs my house rent to fill the tank up."

Sheryl tells him, "It's not that bad. I just budget it like any other bill. It's good on highway miles, but it's horrible in the city."

Terron says, "Yes, this is nice, Sheryl."

Sheryl says, "I see you have a tattoo of a motorcycle on your arm. Do you ride bikes?"

Terron replies, "I do."

Sheryl asks, "How long have you been riding?"

Terron says, "I've been riding for about seven years."

Sheryl says, "I had a friend who would take me to a dirt-bike track called Devil's Dip back home in LA, and we would ride for hours. That was way back in the day. I was about fifteen. I never rode a street bike. A street bike seems as though it would be a much smoother ride."

Terron says, "I do like the street bikes better."

Sheryl says, "When I was younger, I was a tomboy. The dirt-bike track was fun."

Terron says, "A tomboy? I didn't see that coming. If I had to guess, I would have said more like a daddy's girl."

Sheryl replies, "Well, I didn't see my father much. He treated my mother bad, and then he died three days after my sweet sixteen birthday party."

Terron says, "I'm sorry, Sheryl."

Sheryl says, "It's okay. I never really knew him."

Terron says, "Well, I never rode a dirt bike, but yes, I love riding my motorcycle."

Sheryl asks, "What type of motorcycle do you have?"

Terron says, "I have a 2010 Suzuki 1000."

Sheryl asks, "What color is it?"

Terron says, "It's money green and chrome out."

Sheryl says, "That's a nice color scheme."

Terron replies, "Thanks."

Sheryl says, "I want to take a motorcycle course this summer."

Terron says, "I took it. It's a good course to take. It's very informative. I took it after five years of riding and was not aware of a lot of things the course covered. I mean basic stuff like leaning into the corners while keeping your arms straight. Let me know—I'll take the course with you if you're interested."

Sheryl says, "I see so many women riding motorcycles these days. Terron, why do you ride?"

Terron replies, "I like to be free, and it gives me a chance to clear my head."

They drive in silence for a little way, and then Sheryl says, "Wow! Boston Bowl! Now there's something I have not done in a long time. Can you bowl?"

Terron says, "I can beat you."

Sheryl says excitedly, "What? I love bowling. Let's go bowl tonight and catch a movie another time."

Terron says, "It's cool with me. Let's do it. Let me beat your butt, and I don't want to hear any excuses. I don't want to hear nothing about your nails or anything."

They pull into the parking lot and walk in to the attendant's desk. Terron says, "How are you doing?"

The attendant says, "Good, sir. What sizes do you need?"

Terron says, "Can I have two pairs of twelves, please?"

Sheryl snorts. "Mr. Funny Man."

Terron says, "I'm just kidding, sir."

Sheryl says, "I'll order my own shoes. Can I have a pair of size eights, please?"

The attendant says, "What about you, sir?"

Terron says, "Let me have a ten and a half."

Sheryl says, "You know you need that size twelve."

Terron says, "Whatever!"

Sheryl says, "I don't want to hear the excuse that your feet were cramped. Are you competitive?"

Terron asks, "Why? You're not going to beat me."

Sheryl taunts, "You have skills like that?"

Terron says, "I can bowl a little bit. What's your average?"

Sheryl replies, "I don't have an average. I just like bowling. Let's put a bet on it."

Terron says, "If I win, you pay for dinner, because now I'm hungry."

Sheryl says, "Okay, and if I win, you'll pay for dinner. I can get with that, but we both have to bowl over a 125 for the bets to be good."

Terron says, "A 125!"

Sheryl replies, "Yes, a 125!"

Terron says, "I have not bowled in a while. You sound like my boys."

Sheryl tells him, "And I'm going to beat you like one of your boys."

Terron replies, "You got jokes and you're talking trash with it. Don't get mad when I spank that butt, Sheryl."

Sheryl says, "Okay. Don't you get mad or embarrassed either, because you're about to get beat down by a woman."

Terron says, "Let's go. You're first."

Sheryl announces, "Here's strike one." She bowls a perfect strike.

Terron says, "Damn, a strike on your first ball? Are you trying to hustle me?"

Sheryl replies, "Not at all. Come on, it's on. Don't get scared now."

Terron says, "I got this."

Sheryl says, "Look at that. Seven pins down."

Terron says, "I can pick that spare up. Got it! Now, let's see if you can get another strike. It's on you."

Sheryl says, "Excuse me? Watch and learn."

Terron exclaims, "What? Another strike?"

Sheryl says, "That's what it looks like to me. You're not going to win this game, Mr. Terron. It's your turn."

Terron replies, "Here's my strike ball."

Sheryl says, "We'll see . . . three pins, Terron ? You have to do better than that. Can you pick that spare up?"

Terron says, "Of course."

Sheryl laughs and says, "What happened? You still have six pins standing. You do know that it's ten pins per roll, right?"

Terron says, "We have jokes."

Sheryl replies, "Not at all. I'm just checking to make sure you know that you're supposed to get ten pins. Excuse me, it's my turn. Again, watch and learn."

Terron says, "What's going on?"

Sheryl says, "I'm sorry. Is that what they call a turkey, three strikes in a row? It's your turn, Mr. Terron."

Terron says, "Here's my strike now."

Sheryl observes, "Eight pins down this time. Much better. Now pick that spare up. Come on, it's only two pins standing to the left. Oops! You were cheated on that one."

Terron says, "It's on now."

Sheryl says, "Really? Come on, Terron, you're not winning this game. Can you say, 'This game is over, and I would like some Legal Sea Foods, please?' Actually, the bet may be off. You may not bowl 125. Man, can you at least bowl the necessary 125 so you can wine and dine me at Legal's?"

Terron replies, "I think you hustled me."

Sheryl says, "Not at all. I just beat you."

And as it turns out, Sheryl does beat him. She tallies the score and says, "Too bad we have to cut this evening short, but I'm glad you bowled a 128. You can take me to Legal's tomorrow night."

Terron says, "That's cool. Tomorrow evening is good for me. Legal's it is."

Sheryl says, "I look forward to it. I really had a good time tonight. Thanks for the evening. You seem to be a really nice guy. Next time, we'll go out earlier so we can have more time to play."

Terron responds, "I had a nice time as well. I look forward to hanging out with you again. Thanks for giving me the Escalade experience. Call me and let me know you made it in, Sheryl. Thanks."

Sheryl says, "Sure, and thank you again, Terron. Good night."

At mid-afternoon the following day, Sheryl's cell phone rings. "Hello!"

Angie says, "Hey, girl."

Sheryl asks, "What's going on?"

Angie replies, "I just came from the doctor's office."

Sheryl says, "The doctor's office! Well, what did he say?"

Angie says, "I'm actually four months pregnant."

Sheryl screams, "Congratulations! You're not even showing yet."

Angie says, "My doctor said by the end of the sixth or seventh month, I'll be as big as a house."

Sheryl asks, "Is it a boy or girl?"

Angie replies, "I don't know yet. I want to be surprised. I just pray that my baby will be healthy. Everything is falling in place now, one thing after another."

Sheryl says, "I'm so happy for you."

Angie says, "Thank you, girl."

Sheryl says, "Guess what?"

Angie says, "What?"

Sheryl tells her, "I met a new friend."

Angie asks, "What kind of car does he drive?"

Sheryl says, "I didn't notice. I think it's a Grand Am or something like that."

Angie exclaims, "A Grand Am!"

Sheryl says, "Yes, I think that's what it is."

Angie says, "Where did you meet him at?"

Sheryl replies, "Girl, I met him in the gas station. He walked up and started pumping my gas for me, and the conversation took off from there. We went bowling last night and had a good time. We were going to the movies at first, but passed the bowling alley and decided to go bowling instead."

Angie asks, "Is he cute?"

Sheryl says, "He's okay."

Angie says, "I hear you, girl. Well, take your time and don't look for red flags. Give the man a chance."

Sheryl says, "He seems to be very nice, but it's too early to tell."

Angie asks, "What's he like?"

Sheryl says, "I couldn't really tell. I need another date or two with him. I do know that I want a caring and thoughtful, yet rugged man around me. I want a man who will take control and be respectful at the same time."

Angie says, "Did he seem like that type?"

Sheryl replies, "He's more of a 'whatever you want to do' type of guy. That was what he seemed like."

Angie says, "Does he seem like a mama's boy?"

Sheryl says, "I'm not sure yet. Nah, he's not a mama's boy. I can't put my hand on it. It's just something about him I don't trust."

Angie tells her, "Don't look for anything. Just have fun until he gives you reason not to hang with you."

Sheryl replies, "Yeah, I know. I'm always finding a way to get away, huh?"

Angie says, "Just have fun. You'll be okay."

Sheryl says, "Anyway, girl, I'll chat with you later. I need to figure out what I'm eating for lunch. I want some Lenny's."

Angie agrees, "Yes. I haven't had no cocoa bread or a cheese and beef patty in too long."

Sheryl says, "I think I'm going to get me some oxtail, rice, and peas."

Angie says, "That sounds good. Hey, before you go, I wanted to ask you something."

Sheryl says, "What's up?"

Angie asks, "Would you be my child's godparent?"

Sheryl replies, "Of course."

Angie says, "Thanks. You know you're my girl. Can you start thinking of some names? Think of both girls' and boys' names. What time are you off work?"

Sheryl says, "I'm about to leave as soon as I get off this call with you. It's kind of slow in the office. Then I'm going to wash this truck. I'll call you later on."

Angie replies, "Okay. Later for now."

As Sheryl sits in her office, she thinks, "I'm ready to get out of here. Let me clean my station and shut this computer down. Clock out and be out. I'll add a little some to my diary before I leave."

Diary Entry 3:

What's wrong with me? Is it me? Is Angie right? Am I going about searching for love the wrong way? Am I looking for the wrong things in men? Why do I keep trying to groom the guys I meet? I wish there was an answer to this madness. One day I hope to find a solution to my concern.

I guess for now it's the same ol' same ol'. At least I can say I'm healthy. I have a good job and my health. For now, I'll just be happy that I'm blessed with life. I'm out of here. Off to get some food, then maybe do some shopping.

Chapter 6

The Shopping Spree

Sheryl stops by Lenny's Caribbean Restaurant for a Beef Pattie with Cocoa bread and cheese, and then head off to Copley for some afternoon shopping. She enters a boutique called Imani.

Sheryl says to the sales clerk, "Excuse me, do you have this in orange?"

The clerk replies, "I'm sorry, my name is Bruce. Get it right, sister girl. It's right here on my tag. And what's your name?"

Sheryl says, "My name is Sheryl."

Bruce says, "Well, it's nice to meet you, Sheryl. Now what can I do for you?

Let me check on this blouse for you. Hand me that. Yes, this is nice. I'll wear this with some boyfriend jeans and pumps. Because you know my big butt cannot get in no high-ass heels."

Sheryl says, "Bruce, you are too much."

Bruce replies, "I know. I'll be right back. Let me check on this for you." He comes back a few moments later and tells her, "Sheryl, you're in luck. We have three more left. I brought you a medium and a large, just in case you don't like how the medium fits you. Here you go, girl. Try these on, and when you come out, I want you to work it."

Sheryl says, "I am not messing with you."

Bruce says, "For real, I want to see you work it." Sheryl puts on one of the blouses and comes out of the dressing room. "Let me see, girl. That's fitting you nice. Which size is that?"

Sheryl says, "This is the large."

Bruce says, "See? Bruce knows the body, girl, Bruce knows the body. Will this be it for you?"

Sheryl replies, "Yes. I need to find some shoes now."

Bruce says, "Sheryl, there's a European shoe store four stores down on the left. You should check it out and tell them Bruce sent you. They might just hook you up, because I always bring them the business. If that don't work, there's a forum of stores called the Ten Best just ten minutes from here."

Sheryl says, "What do you know about Ten Best?"

Bruce says, "What? I *am* Ten Best. That's where I get all my latest designs and fashions. Yes, I do."

Sheryl says, "Bruce, you are a mess. So am I."

Bruce says, "We should hang out sometime. What side of town do you live on? I'm not too far from here, over by the Charles River. Here's my number. Make sure you call me. I love cooking, girl. We can have girl's night out. I don't do a lot of women either. That's just tacky. Be asking me to wear my clothes and shoes, I tell you, just tacky."

Sheryl says, "Here's my card. Let's do that, hang out sometime and shop."

Bruce says, "I love to shop. Let's do that, because I shop like there's no tomorrow. Okay! Call me, Sheryl, for real."

Sheryl says, "I will. Bye, Bruce, and thanks."

Bruce replies, "Bye, girl."

Sheryl walks down the street to the European shoe store. Browsing their stock, she thinks, "Bruce, where did you direct me to? These shoes are so not me. I need me some sandals. Let me get out of here. I know I could never go wrong with the power of Macy's or the Ten Best." Stepping out, she calls, "Taxi! Yes, uptown to Macy's, please."

Sheryl arrives at Macy's and heads straight to the shoe department. "Good afternoon, sir. How are you doing?"

The sales clerk replies, "Good afternoon. Can I help you find anything?"

Sheryl says, "I went to your website and picked out some sandals I wanted to get. But I forgot my list."

The clerk asks, "Do you remember which sandals they were?"

Sheryl says, "Do you have the season catalog? I picked several of the sandals from there."

The clerk says, "As a matter of fact, we do. Let me grab it for you."

Sheryl, pointing to the catalog images, says, "I need the black Nine West, the red Marc Fisher, the gray Nine West, and the black Anne Klein. All in a size eight narrow, please."

The clerk replies, "Okay. Let me see what we have in stock. I'll be right back."

Sheryl says, "Thank you."

The clerk comes back and says, "We have all of them except the gray Nine West sandals."

Sheryl asks, "Are there any deals for buying more than one pair at a time?"

The clerk says, "I can check for you, but offhand, no. All these are new, and normally the sales won't start for another three months. Let me check on that; I'll be right back."

Sheryl replies, "Thank you."

The clerk returns and tells her, "I'm sorry; actually, we do have a sale. You buy one pair and get the second pair at half price."

Sheryl says, "So I can get two at full price and two more at half price?"

The clerk says, "Yes!"

Sheryl says, "Okay, then I just need to find another sandal that I like. Can you grab . . . that one for me, please?"

The clerk says, "Sure. That's a popular all-purpose sandal. It's a good buy."

Sheryl says, "Then that's it. I'm all set."

The clerk asks, "Is there anything else I can get for you?"

Sheryl replies, "No. That will be it, and thank you. You were a great help."

The clerk rings her up and says, "Have a good night."

Sheryl leaves Copley and decides to get her truck washed. The car wash attendant says, "Hello. What type of wash would you like today?"

Sheryl says, "Hi. Can I have the works package, please?"

The attendant says, "Sure. That will be twenty-two fifty. What type of air freshener would you like?"

Sheryl replies, "Can I have the baby powder fragrance, please?"

The attendant says, "Of course! The detailer will give you your keys as soon as the job is finished. Just hand him your receipt."

Sheryl asks, "This package does come with the tire shine, correct?"

The attendant says, "Yes!"

Sheryl says, "Thank you."

As Sheryl waits for her car to come through the wash belt, she's approached by man who says, "How are you doing?"

Sheryl replies, "I'm fine, and you?"

The man introduces himself, "I'm Dave."

Sheryl says, "Hi Dave, I'm Sheryl."

Dave says, "I see they have your truck looking good."

Sheryl agrees, "It does look good. Thanks."

Dave asks, "Do you always get your car washed here?"

Sheryl says, "I do for the most part. What about you?"

Dave replies, "I do as well."

Sheryl says, "You live in this area?"

Dave tells her, "I stay across the street from Forrest Hills train station. What about you?"

Sheryl says, "I stay over by the Charles River, but I like this car wash here. I've been coming here for years. So, Dave, what do you do when you're not washing your car?"

Dave says, "I write grants and proposals for the mayor's office."

Sheryl asks, "How do you like doing that? That's a really big responsibility."

Dave says, "I enjoy it. I like writing."

Sheryl says, "How long have you been with the city?"

Dave says, "It will be five years next month."

Sheryl asks, "Where did you go to school?"

Dave says, "I went to a business school for office management."

Sheryl says, "Did you go to Burdett Business School?"

Dave replies, "I did. How did you know that?"

Sheryl says, "How many business schools are there in Boston?"

Dave says, "Quite a few, actually."

Sheryl says, "Must have been a lucky guess."

Dave asks, "What about yourself?"

Sheryl replies, "I went to Brown."

Dave says, "Oh, okay. In Providence, right?"

Sheryl says, "Yes!"

Dave says, "So what type of work do you do?"

Sheryl replies, "I'm an accountant."

Dave says, "How do you like working in that field?"

Sheryl says, "I love it. I enjoy working with numbers."

Dave says, "What are you doing after this? Would you like to do something?"

Sheryl says, "I'm about to wax my truck. You can help me if you like."

Dave says, "You just washed it!"

Sheryl retorts, "Yes, and now I have to wax it! You have to get the dirt off first."

Dave says, "Let's do it. I'm not doing anything. Do you like the Legal Sea Foods in Copley?"

Sheryl says excitedly, "What? I do! That's one of my favorite places to eat. I love Legal's."

Dave asks, "Would you like to go there after we wax your truck?"

Sheryl says with no hesitation, "Sure. Sounds like a plan, Dave. Do I have to worry about any crazy girlfriends?"

Dave replies, "I don't know. Have you been dating girls long, Sheryl?"

Sheryl says, "Okay, you got me. That was cute! You have a sense of humor."

Dave says, "But no, I don't have crazy girlfriends you have to worry about. What about crazy and jealous ex-boyfriends?"

Sheryl admits, "I do, but they don't know where you live at."

Dave says, "Huh."

Sheryl says, "I'm just kidding. No jealous exes."

Dave says, "However, you do have to worry about my fifteen—and ten-year-old sisters, whom I need to go check on."

Sheryl replies, "It sounds like they live with you."

Dave says, "They do. We lost our mom about four years ago."

Sheryl says, "I'm sorry to hear that. Are there any more brothers or sisters?"

Dave says, "No. It's just the three of us. I have full custody. They are probably at my house with their girlfriends trying to cook. The fifteen-year-old loves the cooking shows."

Sheryl asks, "Can she cook?"

Dave replies, "She actually can. Her breakfast food is on point."

Sheryl says, "She likes cooking breakfast? Okay, that's a start. What about the younger one?"

Dave says, "She's into the Internet thing. She has a Facebook page and everything."

Sheryl says, "Do you monitor it?"

Dave says, "I sure do, and she hates it. I had to get me a page and request her as family to keep up with her. Do you know she blocked me once?"

Sheryl asks, "What did you do?"

Dave replies, "I told her to friend me back or I would delete her service. She did not like it, but she had no choice. Do you have a Facebook page?"

Sheryl says, "I do, but I'm never on it. I'm mainly online to check my e-mails. Is it hard raising the girls? How do you guys get along?"

Dave says, "We get along pretty good. They listen. I'm fair, and I allow them to be young ladies. I do my best and actually enjoy it."

Sheryl says, "How long have you had custody?"

Dave replies, "I've had custody ever since we lost our mom."

Sheryl says, "Excuse me, Dave, my cell is ringing. Hello?" He waves to her and walks off to check on his sisters.

Angie says, "Hey, it's Angie. What are you doing?"

Sheryl replies, "I'm talking to Dave, a friend I just met at the car wash. We're about to wax our cars, then go eat at Legal Sea Foods at Copley."

Angie says, "Oh, really? That should be nice. I haven't been there in a while. I used to love walking through Copley after work; that mall is nice. Well, I don't want to be rude, so I'll call you back later."

Sheryl says, "You're good. He's checking on his little sisters. He has custody of them."

Angie asks, "How did he get custody?"

Sheryl says, "He lost his mom about four years ago. I guess he has no other relatives here."

Angie says, "That must be tough on him."

Sheryl says, "He said he likes it."

Angie says, "He must have a lot of patience."

Sheryl says, "I don't know, but he is sexy, girl. About five feet nine with a slim build. He wears it well. He writes grants for the mayor's office."

Angie replies, "Okay, so he has a good job."

Sheryl says, "Guess what kind of car he drives?"

Angie says, "Well, with two little sisters, he might be wheeling a minivan."

Sheryl says, "Try a 2006 pearl white convertible Corvette."

Angie says, "Take your time, girl, take your time. What's up with the Wayne guy?"

Sheryl says, "I haven't heard from him. He said he would call when he was thinking about me, so I guess he hasn't been thinking about me."

Angie asks, "Is Dave back yet?"

Sheryl replies, "Not yet."

Angie says, "When you guys get to the mall, check to see if they still have the Sharper Image store there. I want to swing by later on this week and pick up a few hobby items for Roland."

Sheryl says, "I was in the Sharper Image store just the other day. That overpriced store is not going anywhere."

Angie replies, "Okay, cool. Hopefully I can swing by there in the morning before I go to work. Anyway, about time you gave someone a chance, Sheryl."

Sheryl says, "Girl, he's just helping me wax my truck and taking me out to eat. I don't know. We'll see. He is sexy."

Angie says, "Sheryl, I really called you because it seemed like something was on your mind the other night. Is everything okay?"

Sheryl says, "What night are you talking about?"

Angie replies, "Last night, when you were at the new house".

Sheryl says, "I just had some things on my mind. I'm straight. You know being single can be lonely at times, and you and Roland kissing all over each other don't make it any easier. What are you guys doing tonight?"

Angie says, "Roland has a romantic dinner planned at the house. He's off today. I just spoke to him. He was 'setting the stage,' as he calls it, for tonight."

Sheryl says, "Getting the stage set? Angie, let me find out Roland has a little romance."

Angie replies, "He's all romance. He's setting both my bath and the table with my favorites now."

Sheryl asks, "And what are your favorites?"

Angie says, "You know I like a hot bath with bubbles all the way up to the top of the tub, and my dinner table set up with scented candles, sunflowers, white roses, white grapes, exotic fruit, and a cold, tall glass of white zinfandel."

Sheryl says, "I know that's right, Angie."

Angie says, "Hold on. Let me call you back, girl."

Sheryl asks, "What's up?"

Angie replies, "Girl, some fool is pointing a gun at people in the middle of the street over here on Morton. I'll call you back."

Sheryl exclaims, "Huh?"

Angie says, "I'll call you back. I have to go."

Angie calls in a disturbance to dispatch, saying, "This is Detective Angie Coleman calling for backup on the nine hundred block of Morton Street. I have a white, bald, athletically built male, about six feet two inches tall, with a blue T-shirt, blue jeans, and black sneakers, waving a gun in the middle of the street. Again, this is at the nine hundred block of Morton Street."

The dispatcher replies, "Cars are being sent to your location, 10-4."

Angie hangs up her phone and gets out of her unmarked car. She approaches the armed man and says, "Okay, sir! Sir! How are you doing? I'm Detective Coleman, and this is my partner, Detective Patterson. I'm going to ask you to focus on me and lower your gun."

The disturbed man says, "Why would I do that?"

Angie says, "Sir, you will do that so no one will get hurt. You don't really want to hurt anybody. I'm sure whatever it is, we can work it out."

The disturbed man accuses her, "Why are you and your partner pointing your weapons at me? You police are all the same. You just want to hurt people."

Angie replies, "Sir, we're not trying to hurt you or anyone. We just want you to lower your weapon so no one will get hurt."

The disturbed man says, "I don't think I can do that, Miss Police."

Angie orders, "Sir, put the weapon down."

Detective Patterson repeats, "Put the weapon down, sir."

The disturbed man screams out, "Die, police! You all need to die! Die, you pigs!" Then the shots ring out.

Detective Patterson calls in to dispatch and says, "Shots fired, shots fired. I repeat, shots fired."

Angie says, "Patterson, I'm hit. I'm hit. Where's our back up (as Angie runs and dives to shield herself behind her unmarked police car)?

Detective Patterson says, "I'm all your backup now, girl. Stay with me, Angie." Detective Patterson shouts to dispatch, "Officer down, officer down, I repeat, officer down. Send paramedics and backup to the nine hundred block of Morton Street. I repeat: officer down. Send paramedics to the nine hundred block of Morton Street. Angie, stay with me, girl. After we get through this, we both are taking a long vacation on me. Come on, Angie, stay with me. Help is on the way. Help is on the way."

Dave comes out of his apartment and sees the look on Sheryl's face. "Are you okay?"

Sheryl replies, "I don't know. My girl just said some fool was pointing a gun in the middle of the street. Here's my number. Call me later. I have to go."

Dave asks, "Are you sure you're okay? Would you like some company?"

Sheryl says, "No. I'll hit you up later."

Dave tells her, "Okay. Call me if you need to talk. I hope all is okay with your people."

Sheryl says, "All right. I'll speak to you soon."

As Sheryl pulls out of the car wash lot, she calls Roland. Roland answers, "Hello. Who's this?"

Sheryl replies, "This is Sheryl, boy. Where's Angie?"

Roland says, "She's at work."

Sheryl tells him, "I don't want to scare you, but we were just talking on the phone and she said some fool was waving a gun in the street. Then she hung up."

Roland says, "Sheryl, you know that's her job. She's good. If I worry about her job, I'll be a nervous wreck. Believe me, we had these discussions a long time ago. I'm comfortable with it now."

Sheryl says, "This sounded very serious, and she's not answering her phone. Roland, please give her a call and then call me back. Please."

Roland replies, "All right, I'll call her then call you back."

Sheryl pleads, "Call me back, Roland."

Roland says, "All right. I'm out."

An hour goes by. Sheryl decides to call Roland again. "What's going on? Where are you at?"

Roland says, "I'm at City Hospital."

Sheryl exclaims, "Oh, my God, City Hospital?"

Roland says, "My baby got shot two times at close range with a .38 magnum. I'll call you back."

Sheryl screams, "No! I'm on my way. Oh, my God! Please, Lord, let Angie be okay."

Sheryl races through traffic and arrives at City Hospital. From the parking lot, she calls Roland again. "I told her this damn job was dangerous. Roland, you better answer your phone."

Roland answers, "Hello."

Sheryl asks, "Where are you at?"

Roland replies, "I'm in the ER waiting room."

Sheryl says, "I'm here. I'm getting out of the elevator now. Roland, I'm so sorry. How's she doing?"

Roland says, "They don't know yet. She's in critical condition."

Sheryl replies, "Oh, my God, Roland, she had just called me. I was just talking to her. Not Angie, Lord. She's all I have. Please don't take her from me. Please don't." She walks into the waiting room and embraces Roland.

Roland says, "Come on. Let's just pray that she pulls through. I'm so tired of waiting to hear something."

Sheryl says, "Here's a doctor now."

The doctor approaches and says, "Are you here for Detective Coleman? I'm Doctor Smith."

Roland responds, "I'm Roland, her fiancé."

Sheryl says, "I'm Sheryl, her sister. What can you tell us?"

Doctor Smith says, "Well, it's very serious. We removed one of the two bullets and stopped the bleeding. She still has the bullet right under the heart. We're doing everything we can to get her back home to you."

Roland asks, "When can I talk to her?"

Doctor Smith says, "It's premature to say at this time. She's still unconscious. Is there anything I can get you?"

Roland replies, "No; we're all set. We're just going to stay here in the waiting room."

Doctor Smith says, "Okay. I'll make sure someone brings you a blanket to make you as comfortable as possible."

Roland says, "Thank you. Is she breathing on her own?"

Doctor Smith replies, "We're doing the best we can."

Roland prays silently, "Please give my baby back to me, Lord. I love her and need her so much. We have so much living and serving to do."

Roland then says aloud, "Dr. Smith, you have to do your best. I need my wife. She's my everything."

Sheryl says, "Roland, the doctor will let us know as soon as possible."

Roland says, "That's my wife. I need her." The doctor nods sympathetically and leaves them.

Sheryl says, "It's going to be okay. You have to be strong for her. Have you called Angie's parents yet?"

Roland replies, "Yes. They're trying to catch the next flight out of Jamaica as we speak."

Sheryl says, "Jamaica?"

Roland says, "They're on vacation." He adds numbly, "I don't believe my baby is in the hospital."

Sheryl replies, "It's going to be all right, Roland. It's in God's hands now. Here—sit and relax. Just relax, baby! Let me rub your shoulders. Everything is going to be okay. I'll massage your neck and back."

Roland says, "Not right now. I'm good. Sheryl, what's up? Don't touch me like that."

Sheryl says, "Oh, Roland, please don't say that. I envy what you and Angie have. You're a handsome, thoughtful, caring, hardworking man. You're going through a lot at the moment. You deserve to be relaxed. Angie needs you to be strong for her. Let me get you relaxed."

Roland asks, "What do you mean, relaxed?"

Sheryl replies, "You know. Just sit still. I got you."

Roland says, "Have you been drinking?"

Sheryl says, "I just had four nip shots of Johnny Walker Gold" I picked up from the corner store in route here to the hospital.

Roland reprimands her, "How can you drink at a time like this?"

Sheryl says, "Roland, it's just too much for me to handle."

Roland says, "You smell like straight alcohol."

Sheryl asks, "You want some? This can be our secret."

Roland replies, "Sheryl, I don't keep secrets from Angie. Angie is my everything. You know what she means to me. You're tripping. Please go sit over there."

Sheryl insists, "You can have me, Roland."

Roland says, "What?"

Sheryl says, "You don't want me to get you relaxed and keep you warm tonight?"

Roland says, "Hell no. You're tripping for real. I thought you were a true friend to Angie."

Sheryl says, "I am her friend. But I want to help you now. At least let me help you not think about this. This is all a dream. Angie is okay."

Roland replies, "Sheryl, get out of here. Angie is lying in an emergency room getting operated on. I think it will be best for you to just leave right now."

Sheryl says, "All I want is a man to do for me what you have done for Angie."

Roland says, "Please get out of here."

Sheryl says, "Roland, I'm sorry. Can you just hold me, please?"

Roland says, "Girl, you're playing yourself."

Sheryl responds, "Just hold me, Roland. She doesn't have to know. I won't tell her that you were trying to come on to me."

Roland looks at her, confused, and says, "What? Sheryl, if I have to ask you one more time to get out of here, I'm going to have you put out."

Sheryl says, "Tonight your mind needs to be free."

Roland says, "Take your damn hands off me. Do you hear yourself talking? You are truly disrespecting yourself."

Sheryl says, "Sit back and feel me on your lap."

Roland replies, "You have gone crazy! Look at me and read my lips. Angie and I are happy, and my baby is coming home. Our happiness will not be sold to your devil. Get the hell out of this waiting room, and don't come back until you are sober!"

Sheryl says, "You don't mean that, Roland. You're just upset."

Roland says, "Do I need to call security? Just go home, Sheryl."

Sheryl promises, "I'll bring you back your toothbrush and change of clothes."

Roland says, "Don't bring me anything. Just leave."

Six hours later, as the sunlight shines through the glass doors of the hospital, Angie's parents arrive at the waiting room, awakening Roland. Ms. Coleman taps his shoulder and chants, "Roland. Roland. Roland. Wake up. It must been a long night for you, dear."

Roland yawns and stretches. "Good morning, Mr. and Ms. Coleman."

Mr. Coleman replies, "Good morning. What's the update?"

Roland says, "She was shot twice in the chest with a .38. They were able to remove one bullet, but the other one is still lodged under her heart."

Ms. Coleman asks, "Where is Sheryl?"

Roland says, "She'll be back. She went home to grab some things. How was the flight?"

Mr. Coleman says, "It was good. Very smooth."

Ms. Coleman says, "Roland, we thank you for being here for Angie. She told us about the engagement and the new house. How are you holding up?"

Roland says, "I need her to get through this and come home."

Mr. Coleman says, "Have they shared any other information with you?"

Roland says, "Dr. Smith stopped by last night to say that the third-shift nurse would let me know something. I guess she must have decided to let me sleep."

Ms. Coleman says, "I'll be glad when Dr. Smith or someone comes out and tell us something. I'm surprised that Sheryl is not here."

Roland explains, "It was really hard for her. She couldn't handle Angie being here in the hospital, so I told her to go home and get some rest. She should be her shortly."

Dr. Smith walks in the waiting room and says, "Excuse me."

Ms. Coleman cuts him off immediately. "I'm Ms. Coleman and this is my husband. What is going on with our daughter?"

Dr. Smith says, "I'm sorry. There was nothing we were able to do. The bullet under her heart caused severe internal bleeding. We came out of the second surgery ten minutes ago. Your daughter went into cardiac arrest on the operating table, and we couldn't resuscitate her. On behalf of myself and our staff, we are so sorry for your loss. If you have any questions, don't hesitate to ask me. I'm sorry."

Ms. Coleman screams out, "My baby!"

Mr. Coleman embraces his wife and says, "I know, baby. It's hard, but we're going to get through it. We all have to get through this together. Roland, son, we're going to get through this as a family."

Ms. Coleman cries, "*Why*? Why my Angie? She did everything by the Book and was good to you, Lord. Why my baby?"

Roland says, "We were good to each other. What did I do, Lord, to be punished like this? Why me? You took my soul. *Why*? She and my child were all I had to live for. You took my family from me. What did I do to deserve this, Lord?"

Ms. Coleman gasps. "Roland, no."

Roland says, "Yes! She was four months pregnant. We have to pray together. We're still a family. You guys are all I have."

Mr. Coleman says, "Son, we'll get through this. I promise, we'll get through this".

Sheryl walks into the waiting room and sees the scene of grief. She has an immediately breakdown. "*Nooo*! Please tell me it's not so! Angie is not gone! She can't be; she's my only friend. Lord, I promise I'll do right. I'll do right. Mr. and Ms. Coleman, I'm so sorry."

Ms. Coleman replies, "You don't need to apologize. With her line of work, following in her father's footsteps, we prepared for this a long time ago, even though we prayed that this day will never come."

Mr. Coleman says, "Listen, Roland and Sheryl, we have to be here for each other and lend that ear whenever it's needed. You know how to reach us. Call anytime. My wife and I are going back to our hotel to start making preparations."

Roland says, "Yes, sir."

Mr. Coleman says, "It's going to be hard. Just know she's in a better place now. We'll go over the arrangements and everything else later."

Roland replies, "No problem, sir."

Mr. Coleman says, "I'll speak with you guys shortly."

Sheryl leaves the hospital. En route to her condo, she gets a call. "Hello!"

Ms. Coleman says, "Hey, Sheryl, are you okay, baby?"

Sheryl replies, "Yes, I'm okay. Thank you for calling me. I feel so empty and lost. Ms. Coleman, I don't understand. Angie practiced living by the Book. She worked hard, she didn't smoke, and she kept me in line. I really don't understand why she was taken from us."

Ms. Coleman replies, "Baby, the Lord works in mysterious ways. Just know that she served her purpose here on earth. We're attempting to make the arrangements for the wake this Saturday at noon. I'll let you know the arrangements as soon as I can."

Sheryl replies, "Okay, Ms. Coleman. Thank you. If you need anything before Saturday, just call me. How's Mr. Coleman doing?"

Ms. Coleman says, "He's doing okay. Stubborn like normal, but he's okay. I want you to keep the family, Roland, and yourself in prayer."

Sheryl says, "Yes, Ms. Coleman."

Ms. Coleman says, "I'll talk to you later. Bye-bye."

Sheryl replies, "Bye!"

As the conversation ends, Sheryl arrives home. She pulls out her diary and begins to write.

Diary Entry 4:

Today is May 4th, 2012, and I'm alone. My best friend is gone. Being the last one of her friends to talk to her before her death has me feeling like the biggest fool.

I mean did I really try to have sex with her man at his weakest point, while my best friend was lying in a hospital bed? Come on, now. How low can a person get? The wake is this Saturday, and I'm really feeling some type of way.

I still have not spoken with Roland regarding my actions. However, I have to do it and face the music. He must really hate me. Angie told me to give my friend Wayne a chance, so I'm going to give Wayne a chance. He never called me. I hope he remembers me. He seems like a really nice guy.

I wonder what Dave is doing. He seems like a nice guy as well, but he's not really my type. He is a little tight for me.

What would Angie do in this situation? Who would interest her? I know she would probably go for Wayne. He's more down to earth and seems like he gets along with everyone. Angie would say, "Sheryl, he's a hard worker and he would make time for you.

That man really likes you. You should make time for him and stop looking for someone to pimp you as opposed to loving you."

Yes, I can hear her voice now. "Trust your heart. Have faith. Believe in love and not the dollar all the time. Everybody is not out to get you, girl." Wow,

My girl was crazy and beautiful at the same time. I miss you, Angie, and I will always love you. I'll see you at the wake, girl. Your best friend forever, Sheryl (I love you XOXOXOXOX).

Chapter 7

The Rehab

Two months have passed since the funeral and things are almost back to normal. Sheryl is just leaving work for the day and runs into Roland coming out of Store 24 in Mattapan Square. "Hey, Roland. How are you doing?"

Roland replies, "I'm good, and you?"

Sheryl says, "I'm okay. You know, I never got the chance to say that I was sorry for acting out and making a complete butt of myself. I'm so sorry."

Roland says, "It's okay. I'm good. I guess it don't matter now, right?"

Sheryl says, "It does matter. I tried to prove a very childish point that was not necessary. Roland, you are a good man, and my girl was blessed to have you. I hope you can forgive me and at least accept my apology. Maybe we can be friends."

Roland says, "That's cool. Thanks. I needed to hear that from you. How are you holding up? Are you okay?"

Sheryl replies, "I'm managing. I do have my weak points, but I manage to get through. If you ever need to talk, I'm here for you. I know how much you loved Angie."

Roland says, "I appreciate that, Sheryl."

Sheryl says, "Don't you dare be a stranger. I'm serious."

Roland says, "I got you."

Sheryl asks, "What are you doing now?"

Roland tells her, "I'm about to get me a lottery ticket and head back to the house."

Sheryl says, "Do you mind taking a walk with me? I just want to talk."

Roland replies, "Sure, that's cool. Let me get my lottery ticket and a Sprite. Would you like anything?"

Sheryl says, "Nah, I'm good. I'll wait for you out here."

Roland goes into the store and comes out again a few minutes later. "Okay, what's up?"

Sheryl replies, "I just have a lot of things on my mind that I never had a chance to share with Angie. You know she was my best friend since college, and we shared so much. And I also want to apologize for my attempts to get Angie to see you as a dog."

Roland says, "Do you really think that all men are dogs?"

Sheryl says, "Well, you proved my theory wrong, and again I'm sorry. At this stage in my life, I need to get right for me."

Roland asks, "Why did you think I was a dog?"

Sheryl says, "It wasn't you; it was men, period. I've had nothing but bad experiences all my life dealing with men, starting with my father. I watched my father abuse my mother. He sold her body for money and drugs. I loved my father dearly, but he was never around, and he had me confused. The last time I saw him was on my sweet sixteen birthday. He died shortly afterward."

Roland says, "I'm sorry to hear that."

Sheryl continues, "I saw him on my thirteenth birthday. He brought me a jacket and gave me twenty dollars. And I saw him in passing when I was ten, in a store called Zody's in Los Angeles. He didn't even recognize me.

"I don't know, Roland. I thought for a long time that the role of men was to be the head of the household, play sports, fight, work on cars, have babies by different women, and pay child support. I guess I never took men seriously because my father bounced in and out of my life. And when he was around, he showed me so much that was negative.

"My father shared one thing that I clearly remember, and that was to work hard for everything I want and not to allow a man to give me nothing unless I decided I wanted it. I was led to believe that a man was out to get what he wanted to get and could get.

Angie use to tell me all this crazy stuff, like to balance my mind, or that I was lonely, frustrated, stubborn with a 'my way or no way' attitude, or that I was just mean to men. Roland, she even told me that I needed to get me some dick!"

Roland exclaims, "What? My baby said that?"

Sheryl says, "Yes! She sure did."

Roland repeats, "*Angie* told you that?"

Sheryl says, "Yes! Your boy Earl was going to get all this, but I can never be number two, so I acted out. Angie was always telling me about myself. She told me I should be tired of taking cold showers, playing with my toys, and buying expensive batteries, because I was always in her business, trying to get her to follow my lead."

Roland asks, "Were you?"

Sheryl says, "I was. But she was right. That's why I wanted to have this talk with you. Your girl Angie never went against the grain, and she always had your back. Every time I would attempt to fill her head with something negative, she would read me and tell me about myself. Roland, I think I want to seek counseling for how I feel toward men. I think I may need some closure on some past events in my life.

"I really think all men are dogs. I never thought that not having a father around would have such an impact on my life. You know, I did some research on children in fatherless home. For example, did you know that fatherless children are five times more likely to commit suicide? And twenty times more likely to show behavior disorders?

"I can relate to these stats. This is why I want to get help."

Roland says, "I feel the same way about some things that are going on in my life. I'm having a hard time dealing with my baby not being here. I don't have my father here either, so I can relate to exactly what you're talking about as far as seeking help."

Sheryl asks, "You don't think I'm crazy or just talking?"

Roland replies, "Not at all. I hear you, and I need to seek some help as well. Do you have any doctors in mind?"

Sheryl says, "I don't. Maybe we can use the same doctor."

Roland says, "That's cool with me. Angie's job has something in place for me. I'll check to see what this therapist is like. If he's any good, I'll refer you to him."

Sheryl says, "That sounds good. Let's set that up. Give me a call when you find something out, or if you just want to talk."

Roland promises, "I'll do that."

Sheryl says, "I'm going to practice taking care of me. I actually have a date this evening. I have a friend named Wayne whom Angie told me to give a chance. I'm going to do that. He has a job and a great relationship with his parents, and he respects me as a woman."

Roland says, "You have to start off with a clean slate, Sheryl. Let it develop."

Sheryl says, "I'll get to know him as the man he is. Who knows? Maybe we'll get the chance to really get to know each other. I may even send him to you for some man pointers."

Roland chuckles. "Check you out."

Sheryl says, "I'm cooking dinner for him tonight, so I need to go home and set up the table. Can you do me a favor?"

Roland asks, "What's that?"

Sheryl says, "Can you help me set the table up as Angie would like it? I've never been a romantic and don't know what it should look like."

Roland responds, "I got you. Are you ready now? If so, we need to pick up some things so we can hook your table up. You mean to tell me you have a friend who is actually getting through those walls of concrete?"

Sheryl replies, "Yes! Thanks to you and my girl Angie. I understand now what it means to know yourself before you can try to make someone else happy."

Roland says, "I hear you, girl. I guess you're ready. Let's go set the mood for you and your friend. Who would have thought that bitter gets better?"